MW01673698

THE BIG MONEY SQUEEZE

THE BIG MONEY $QUEEZE

ADVENTURES IN FOURTH GRADE MONEY MAKING

RYMER STRAUSS

Forbes | Books for Kids

Copyright © 2023 by Rymer Strauss.

All rights reserved. No part of this book may be used or reproduced in any manner whatsoever without prior written consent of the author, except as provided by the United States of America copyright law.

Published by Forbes Books, Charleston, South Carolina.
Member of Advantage Media.

Forbes Books is a registered trademark, and the Forbes Books colophon is a trademark of Forbes Media, LLC.

Printed in the United States of America.

10 9 8 7 6 5 4 3 2 1

ISBN: 979-8-88750-112-3 (Hardcover)
ISBN: 979-8-88750-113-0 (eBook)

LCCN: 2023903802

Cover design by Matthew Morse.
Layout design by Matthew Morse.

This custom publication is intended to provide accurate information and the opinions of the author in regard to the subject matter covered. It is sold with the understanding that the publisher, Forbes Books, is not engaged in rendering legal, financial, or professional services of any kind. If legal advice or other expert assistance is required, the reader is advised to seek the services of a competent professional.

Since 1917, Forbes has remained steadfast in its mission to serve as the defining voice of entrepreneurial capitalism. Forbes Books, launched in 2016 through a partnership with Advantage Media, furthers that aim by helping business and thought leaders bring their stories, passion, and knowledge to the forefront in custom books. Opinions expressed by Forbes Books authors are their own. To be considered for publication, please visit **books.Forbes.com**.

To all the cool kids in the world
who are hopefully inspired to write great books
and start fun companies.

CONTENTS

FOREWORD

The call of entrepreneurship is one that can be heard at any age, whether you're eight or eighty! It's only those bold, daring, and creative individuals who take up stakes and follow their dream that become entrepreneurs.

Rymer Strauss is one of these people. At nine years old, he took a risk and wrote a book that would encourage other young, budding entrepreneurs to take up the flag of free enterprise and try their hand at running their very first business.

It's uplifting to see young people seize the opportunity to learn about business—to learn how to run a company no matter what size and make money. Entrepreneurship and free enterprise can be remarkable forces for good in the world. To see the next generation embracing entrepreneurship is a positive thing for all of mankind.

The publication of *The Big Money Squeeze* marks the launch of Forbes Books for Kids. This is the first of many books designed to educate and inspire young people of the merits (and fun) of entrepreneurship and the free enterprise system. My great hope is that Rymer's book and those forthcoming from Forbes Books for Kids will serve as seeds that help catalyze our next generation of entrepreneurs!

Adam Witty
CEO, Forbes Books

ACKNOWLEDGMENTS

First and foremost, I would like to thank my dad and stepmom, Becky, who taught me to read. They encouraged me to read anything and everything, and they introduced me to new and great books all the time. I want to thank them for also introducing me to business and entrepreneurship at an early age and for always supporting my wild and crazy business ideas.

I want to thank Adam Witty, who once misspelled my name despite being a close family friend, barely beat me in basketball despite being six foot seven and playing a kid, but, most importantly, gave the ultimate green light for this great project that will hopefully inspire more readers, entrepreneurs, and creative spirits.

I sort of acknowledge my older brothers, Colin and Quinn, for being pretty cool and not beating me up too much. I want to also acknowledge my little sister, Penny, who is really fun to play with and isn't too annoying, and my mom.

I want to thank Mrs. Kristin Hackler for spending so much time with me on this project and helping build out a great storyline. And to Mrs. Heidi Scott and Mrs. Kerrie Robertson for all their support to make this book happen.

I want to thank all my buddies at Sea Pines Montessori Academy in Hilton Head for being such great classmates and friends. And I can't forget all of my cousins, especially Gray, Hill, and Charlie, who are really fun and the best cousin buddies ever!

ABOUT THE AUTHOR

Rymer J. Strauss is a nine-year-old boy born and raised on Hilton Head Island in South Carolina. He attends Sea Pines Montessori Academy, where he is currently in fourth grade with some of the coolest kids in the world.

Rymer is an avid reader, sports enthusiast, and creative adventurer. Between reading *Diary of a Wimpy Kid* (a copy of which can be found in every family car) or *Dog Man*, he plays soccer, runs cross-country, is learning judo, and loves swimming. He spends his summers at Camp Mondamin in North Carolina engaged in activities such as mountain climbing, camping, and ziplining. He also loves exploring the world and has sailed with his family in Tortola, skis in Colorado every winter, and has been to Canada, Hawaii, and, of course, to LEGOLAND, where he spends way too much time with the master builders.

After successfully building nearly every LEGO ever created, he recently took on the task of building the Death Star, and amazingly, six months later, neither his little sister nor any of his brothers or friends has managed to damage it at all!

When he's not in school, reading, playing sports, or traveling, he likes to create new business opportunities, tell jokes, and design secret hideouts, lofts, and forts. He's currently working on design plans for a DNA-required access port to his hidden reading nook.

CHAPTER 1

EMPTY POCKETS AND BIG DREAMS

It's raining. And on a great July afternoon too. What a bummer.

To make matters worse, it's hot and humid, and there's lightning. The storm is so bad that Rymer, Ollie, Nia, and Ash can't even go swimming to cool off.

Cooped up in their huge, three-story LEGO treehouse complete with trapdoors and a slide, the best friends sit and sulk as the rain pounds on the roof. Rymer and Ollie are both sitting on beanbags. Rymer's dark-brown hair is all that they can see because his head is bent over a book, reading as usual. His tattered book looks like it's been read a hundred times. Knowing Rymer, it probably has.

Ollie is trying to see how many Goldfish crackers he can stuff into his mouth at once. The others aren't looking at him because he always chews with his mouth open. It's disgusting. And the fact that his sandy-brown hair always looks unbrushed doesn't help. Crumbs keep falling into his hoodie and down his neck, which doesn't seem to bother him one bit. Ollie has an adopted brother, Anthony, who is several years older than him, and two younger siblings, John and Millie, who are both much younger than Ollie. She is with him most of the time and part of the group most days when she's not at ballet practice.

Nia and Ash are sitting next to each other on the bunk bed. Nia (whose name rhymes with Maya) is polishing her two samurai swords with the corner of her T-shirt. She wears the swords everywhere in a sling that goes over her shoulders. The boys used to think it was weird until they learned that she is a real-life descendant of actual, true samurai warriors. She even has a ninja training course in her backyard, but they can't use it in the rain. She is an only child, has an Airedale terrier named Terrence, and lives with her mom, dad, and grandma.

Ash's mom is deaf, so he knows how to use sign language. Everyone in the group wants to learn it because then they could talk without anyone else knowing what they are talking about, except Ash's mom, of course. They have learned a few signs so far for words like "play," "smelly," "hungry," "let's go," "eat," "run," "hide," and "attack."

Ash's blond curls bob up and down as he fiddles with the few LEGO bricks that are left over from when they built this super amazing dream treehouse. They worked for two years gathering enough LEGO bricks for the treehouse, and then they took another year to build it in Rymer's backyard. This means they've been working on this project since they were in first grade.

It's complete with a rope ladder, zipline, and even solar panels from Ash's Technix collection to power the lights. The kids would even love to spend the night there, but they get scared at night. Well, all of them except Nia, who is never afraid of anything. They do have flashlights on both floors, but that's not enough to keep them there after dark for long.

The first floor (which is really the ground) is where they keep anything too big to bring up. Ash and Ollie keep their bikes there. Rymer prefers a scooter. And Nia refuses to ride a bike or a scooter because samurai run all the time to train. The kids can either climb the twisty stairs and go in through a trapdoor in the floor or climb a ladder that hangs off the balcony. To get down, they can go the same way, or they can do something more fun. The second floor has a zipline that goes to the middle of the yard, and the third floor has a huge water slide that lands in the pool behind the house. The third floor also has a fireman pole to the second floor.

Inside, they have a minifridge with snacks, soda, juice boxes, and sometimes chocolate milk. They have a stash of Goldfish crackers, gummy snacks, cookies, and apples. There is also a candy dispenser hanging from the ceiling, but it always seems to be empty. There are big pillows and beanbags everywhere to lie on. There is a punching bag so they can train. There are also a ton of books, maps, games, and—in case they need to blow off steam—Nerf guns and water balloons.

You'd think that would be enough to keep anyone happy. But rainy days are rainy days no matter what.

They all live on the barrier island called George Island, so it's very common to have tropical storms in the late summer and early fall. They would go inside, but none of them want to be around the adults all day. Adults just talk about adult stuff, play weird music, make the kids clean up messes, and eat snacks at a table with a placemat. They would rather lounge around wherever they want and eat the snacks they snuck into the treehouse.

Ash drops the LEGO bricks on the bed and says, "Ahh! It's so boring! Boring!" He would go home, but he's secretly afraid of lightning, and he won't leave the treehouse until it stops. His house is the farthest away from Rymer's, and he wishes he lived next door like Ollie. Ollie and Rymer have a not-so-secret passageway that they dug through the ground between their houses. Both sides are hidden with trapdoors under the bushes.

"I know. I hate rainy days," adds Ollie. "There's nothing to do."

After sitting for another moment in silence, Nia finishes polishing her sword and slides it behind her back into the sling. Knowing that Rymer always has good ideas, she waves her hand in front of his face. "Earth to Rymer," she says.

Nobody is surprised when he blinks and jolts up from the pages of his book and says, "Oh, hey! Is it still raining?"

Ollie face-palms. "Of course it's still raining. My dad said it's going to be raining all weekend."

Ash snaps his fingers. "I know! Let's build something!"

"I'm done building things for a while." Ollie sighs. "I just want to be lazy today. I wish there was a way we could just sit here and play video games. Too bad we don't have a TV in here or anything."

Rymer drops his book on the floor. "Why not?" He stands up from his beanbag chair. "We could put it right there in the corner on top of the minifridge!"

Nia pulls a sword out of the sling and spears an apple from the dish next to the fridge. As she takes a big, juicy bite, she says, "How on earth are we supposed to do that?" Juice drips down her chin in little drops, which she ignores.

Ollie looks up at the solar-powered lights and wonders to himself if they could power anything else.

Ash notices and asks, "Do you think the solar panels could power a TV?"

Rymer says, "Yeah, and what about a gaming console? If we had one, we would have something to do here in the treehouse when it rains. Then we wouldn't have to go inside and get kicked off by Steve and Branson." These are Rymer's two older brothers, and they get kind of mean sometimes.

"Yeah," says Nia. "They never let us play. I wish I was a hundred feet tall. Then I could take it away from them for a change."

The boys laugh at this. She is already several inches taller than the rest of them and stronger too. She is always wishing she was taller or heavier or faster so that she could fight people who are bigger than the others. If she had her way, she would be a giant.

"But seriously, why not? How much money do you all have? Maybe we can go buy one!" Rymer says, getting excited.

They realize pretty quickly that they don't have more than a few dollars between them. They just spent everything they'd saved on the

LEGO bricks to finish their treehouse. Their pockets have nothing but moths in them—as a matter of fact, Ollie quite literally has a dead moth in his. He captured it that morning, accidentally killed it, and wants to have a funeral for it when it stops raining. (Most likely, though, he'll forget about it, and his mom will find it in the dryer after she washes his pants. She's always finding worms, crickets, and other bugs in there, all shriveled and dried up.)

They certainly can't ask their parents for money. Their allowances are already spent through their early teenage years. They need a plan, a way to make money quickly.

Just then, Rymer's little sister, Molly, comes running up the back stairs into the treehouse. She's soaking wet and her makeup is especially messy today from the rain. She's short, cute, and a perfect mix of tomboy and girly girl. She reminds everyone of Jessie from Toy Story. She's smiling from ear to ear despite being soaking wet. She just turned six, and Rymer generally likes playing with her but finds her annoying when his friends want to hang. She's got jean shorts with cool rips on one side and a sparkly pink T-shirt. Her flip-flops have unicorns on them, and they drip water onto the LEGO floor.

Rymer starts to tease her by saying, "Hey, no girls allowed!"

Ollie and Ash join in, but Nia quickly stands up. "Hey, guys. Did you forget I'm a girl? Come on in, Molly. Girl power!" They fist-bump.

"No babies allowed," Rymer teases Molly.

The other boys join in and say, "No babies allowed! No babies allowed! No babies allowed!" And they all laugh.

Molly gets mad and punches Rymer in the stomach, but because she's so little, it doesn't hurt. They all just laugh some more.

"Hey, guys," says Nia. "I'm curious why Molly is so excited." She turns to Molly and asks, "Why did you run through the pouring rain? What were you going to tell us?"

Molly takes a minute to catch her breath, and then she says, "My Barbie Dream House is here! Remember the one Kristi gave me for my birthday present, but she had to order it because it was out at the store? You remember, don't you?"

Kristi is Rymer and Molly's stepmom. She always wears really cool cowgirl boots and promises she will share them with Molly when she gets older.

Molly continues, her voice getting louder. "It's the newest one! This means it's the biggest one too. It has an elevator, a pool, like five floors … you have to see the box. It's huge! I need help opening it. Come on!"

Nia stands up and says, "Sure, Molly. I'll use my swords to open it. Come on, guys."

The boys don't want to leave the treehouse, but they are bored, and the four always stick together. If Nia is going, they are all going. Rymer realizes as they all start to climb down that if the Barbie Dream

House is as big as Molly describes it, they could probably use the cardboard box for something … something big! As they run toward the house, he calls out, "Hey, Nia, don't destroy the cardboard."

He knows they can use it for something when it stops raining. He smiles, thinking of a new idea.

CHAPTER 2

LIGHT BULB!

The kids run through the back door into the house and crash into the living room where Molly's massive box is sitting. Molly drags the box onto a rug with a little help from Nia, and Nia whips her swords out. She slices the tape holding the box closed, and the top pops open.

Rymer says, "Be careful! We want that cardboard to stay in one piece!"

Nia giggles as she stabs the corner of the cardboard box just a little bit and looks at Rymer with a mischievous smile. Rymer glares at her, knowing what she's trying to do. Totally oblivious to them, Molly starts to pull the Dream House out of the box, with no success.

It is stuck in there like glue. She sits down on the floor and crosses her arms with a grunt.

Ash says, "Hey, Nia, why don't you slice the tape along the side? It should just pop open. Pop open!"

She does. And it does! The box falls into a long, flat sheet of cardboard. The house stands on top of it, all pink, white, and plastic.

Molly jumps to her feet and squeals loudly with delight. "You've got to help me take it up to my room now! You've just got to! Let's go! Let's go! Let's go!"

The gang laughs as each one of them grabs a corner of the house. They carefully haul it up the stairs. The whole time, Molly is jumping around and getting in the way. She is so excited that she trips on the top stair and falls face first onto the floor.

She pops up and says, "I'm okay. But I think my loose tooth is more loose now. Hey, guys, did you know I have a loose tooth? It's my first one!" She wiggles it with her finger to show them how loose it is. It almost flops outside her mouth.

They grin at her and set the house down in her room. Rymer smiles, pats her on the head, and says to the gang, "Let's go back to the treehouse. I have an idea. I have to get something, so I'll meet you there in a minute. Grab that box on your way out."

When the group is all back in the treehouse, Rymer sets down a box of markers that he brought from the house and leans the box up against the wall. He writes "The Game Plan" on it. He moves aside so they can read it. They look at him in confusion.

"What game?" Ollie asks. "What are you doing?"

Rymer says, "Hear me out. Listen up. Here's the plan. Listen very, very carefully. I'm only going to say this once—"

Ash knows that he's just being silly and says, "Get to the point, Rymes! To the point!"

Rymer laughs too. Then he explains that this is going to be the brainstorm board for their next big plan. They are going to get a big TV and a gaming system for the treehouse!

Nia says, "That sounds pretty expensive. We don't have that kind of money!"

Rymer says, "That's the fun of it! We're going to start a business and make the money!"

Just then, there is a knock at the door. Ollie opens it to find their friends Sam, Matt, and Isabelle waiting outside.

"Hey, guys!" says Ollie. "What are you doing here?"

Isabelle says, "We were biking past your house, and we heard Molly squealing. We wondered what was going on. Nobody answered the front door, so we figured you were all back here."

Matt climbs into the room. As he glances around, he points at the box and says, "What's that?"

As she flops onto the bunk bed, Nia says, "Oh, that. It's Rymer's next crazy idea. He thinks we can earn enough money to buy a TV and a gaming system. He's finally gone nuts."

Rymer scratches his head and says, "I think we could do it. We just have to figure out a way to make money. How hard could it be?"

"My older sister babysits, and she gets paid a ton of money," Sam says.

"That's a good idea!" Rymer says as he writes "Babysitting" on the cardboard with the markers he brought up.

Ollie says, "I don't know if we're old enough to babysit, guys. I mean, I still have to get babysat."

Rymer crosses "Babysitting" out. "Any other ideas? My dad always says, 'You miss 100 percent of the shots you don't take.' Not really sure what that means, but maybe it will inspire some of you."

"I like baking bread," Isabelle says with some hesitation.

Matt says, "We could sell LEGO art."

Nia says, "We could mow lawns."

Rymer writes "Bake Sale," "Sell Art," and "Mow Lawns" on the Game Plan board.

They decide that baking bread would be too complicated since none of them are allowed to turn on the oven. They don't have any LEGO bricks left after building the treehouse. And they realize that none of them are strong enough to push a lawnmower. All three ideas are crossed out.

Rymer says, "I know! Everyone around here has a dog, it seems like. We could walk dogs."

Rymer writes "Dog Wa" before Ollie screams, "Noooo!"

Something flips in his brain, and he curls up in the corner and starts repeating, "No dog. No dog. No dog."

Nia stands up and takes the marker from Rymer. She crosses "Dog Wa" out and says, "Don't you remember that dog that bit him last year? We will not be walking any dogs."

The group all looks down, trying to think. After sitting there in complete silence for a while, the walkie-talkie beeps. It's Rymer's dad. "Hey, guys, it's getting late. Come on down now."

The kids agree to keep brainstorming for their business and meet back up in the morning. They all say their goodbyes and head home.

As Rymer washes his hands before dinner, he looks around the house and wonders if he could sell anything. "I know people used to make soap. How hard could that be?" He looks at a painting on the wall and thinks, "That could be easy. We could sell our art. It's just splotches of paint. That would be super easy." He sees a bowl of vegetables on the table and thinks, "We could be gardeners and sell carrots and potatoes and stuff. How long does it take to grow a carrot?"

Just as the family begins to eat, Molly gags.

Rymer says, "Come on, Molly, the food isn't that bad!"

His stepmom, Kristi, giggles and says, "So you're not a fan of apples?"

Molly gasps and coughs and sputters. "No! My tooth just fell out, and I almost swallowed it!" She spits it onto the plate.

Rymer's face lights up. He has possibly the best idea yet!

CHAPTER 3

EASY MONEY FROM THE TOOTH FAIRY

Rymer quickly finishes his breakfast the next morning and asks to be excused from the table. His stepmom says, "You can go play with your friends now, but be back for lunch."

When he gets to the treehouse, Rymer writes down "Opperashun Baby Teeth" under "Dog Wa" on the Game Plan board.

Nia climbs into the treehouse and says, "Wait a second, I don't think that's how you spell 'operation.'"

Rymer replies, "That doesn't matter. All that matters is that you get the point."

Ash comes in next and looks confused. "Um, excuse me, Rymer, but I'm not sure that you spelled 'operation' right."

Rymer sighs dramatically and explains again how that isn't important. Ollie comes in eating a bagel with cream cheese and sits on a beanbag. He doesn't say a word because his mouth is full, and he doesn't even notice what's new on the board. Now that all the friends are there, Rymer explains his plan.

He says, "Operation Baby Teeth is a plan to remove all our baby teeth so that we can get money from the tooth fairy. The only problem with this plan is that I don't really know how to take out baby teeth other than just tying the tooth to a door and slamming it. So I need ideas."

Nia crinkles her brow and says, "But how will we eat if we don't have any teeth?"

Rymer says, "I thought about that too. But since they are baby teeth, we know that our adult teeth will just grow back. We can eat soft food until then, like applesauce and yogurt. How long could it take anyway? So anyone have ideas on how to get these teeth out?"

The kids all imagine themselves with no teeth, and they giggle.

Ollie has his hand up first, and he jumps up and down saying, "Ooh, ooh. Pick me. Pick me."

Rymer points at him. Ollie says, "Remember my super powerful toy monster truck I got for my birthday? Well, me and Ash were just tricking it out to make it go faster by taping a cola bottle onto it and shaking it up. That might work!"

Rymer replies, "Great idea! Let's try that first."

Ollie runs home to get his monster truck, and the friends meet in Rymer's backyard. Ash helps Ollie attach the bottle with duct tape, and once it's taped down, they shake the whole thing up. But then they realize that they don't have any string.

Ash looks around and sees the rope that the tire swing is hanging from. It's a little frayed. "I wonder if we could use this," he says, pulling the frayed end.

"No, it's too thick," Nia says. "It won't fit around our teeth. We need something thinner, like fishing line."

Rymer turns to Nia and asks, "Doesn't your dad fish?"

"Yes!" she says, jumping to her feet. "I'll be right back."

As the boys wait for her to run home, they have fun taking turns with the remote control to see who can get the truck to go the fastest.

Nia comes back with the fishing line and a little pair of scissors and says, "Okay. Who wants to go first?"

Rymer decides that since it was his idea, he should probably go first. Ash ties the fishing line to Rymer's front tooth and double knots it.

Ollie holds the remote control, waiting to start, and Nia cuts the bottle tip as Ollie presses full throttle on the control. Zoooom! The truck drives off, and Rymer, in an instant, is pulled forward and covered in fizzy soda until the bottle runs out. The monster truck barely moves. He stands up with the fishing line still dangling and says, "Maybe we should try it again, but I'll run alongside for a minute to get the speed up."

After using up three bottles of cola, Rymer is covered in grass stains and a few bruises and dripping in soda. He feels inside his mouth and frowns when he realizes he still has all of his teeth.

Ash decides to tie himself to the tree with some paracord that he had tied to his bike. They set everything up, and Nia pops off the tip of the bottle. Zooooom! Again, the truck speeds up and then starts spinning its wheels. Ash screams in pain. Nia cuts the string with her sword, and the truck zips away. The friends gather around Ash to see if he's okay.

He says, "I'm okay. It just hurt for a second. Thanks for cutting that string, Nia."

"No problem," she replies as she tucks her sword back in the sling.

"How about pulling our teeth with pliers?" says Ollie. "I saw that in a movie once. In a movie!"

The kids run into the garage and find a heavy pair of pliers on the workbench that Rymer's dad uses sometimes. "Who's first?" Rymer asks, holding them up.

"I'll go," says Ollie. "It was my idea."

He opens his mouth wide so that Rymer can fit the pliers inside it, but Rymer pauses. "Which tooth should I start with?" he asks.

Ollie keeps his mouth open and says, "It uzn't atter. Shush oo it!"

Rymer shrugs, places the pliers around one of Ollie's front teeth, and yanks. The pliers slip off the tooth as Ollie moans a little.

He tries again, clamping the pliers tighter. The pliers slip off again, and Ollie yelps. "That hurt," he says.

"Maybe if I do one in the back," Rymer says. "Open really wide."

Ollie does, and Rymer picks a molar way in the back. He reaches in with the pliers and begins to clamp down, but Ollie screams and pulls away. "That was my tongue!" he says. "Don't you know what you're doing?"

"No!" Rymer yells back. "I'm not a dentist. Why don't you do it yourself?" He throws the pliers on the ground with a little huff of frustration.

"Guys, it's obvious pliers aren't going to work," says Ash. "Our teeth are too slippery. We need to think of something that will stick to them really good."

They think for a minute, and then Ollie says, "What about caramel? I have a bunch of it left over from my birthday party. My grandma made it. My mom always says it will rot our teeth out."

"Yes!" the kids yell. They all take off to Ollie's house, Ash and Ollie on bikes, Rymer on his scooter, and Nia running as always. She adds with a smile, "If I'm going to eat all that candy, I'll have to train extra today."

After stuffing their mouths full of caramel, the kids realize that the candy eventually dissolves in their mouth. Even when they try to mold it around their teeth and pull, it just makes a sticky mess.

"Okay. Well, that didn't really work," says Rymer. "What should we try now?"

"I think we should go back to the treehouse and think some more. My jaw hurts really bad right now," responds Ash.

The group agrees and makes their way back to the treehouse, picking at their teeth and wiping sweet dribbles off their chins. When they get there, they start to brainstorm another plan to get their teeth out.

"I know! We could … actually, I don't know," Rymer says, dropping the markers and plopping down on the bunk bed.

"Let's do something else," Nia says. "I'm tired of thinking about teeth."

"Yeah. Let's decide what kind of gaming system to buy when we get the money," Ollie suggests. "I was thinking we could have Rymer's dad think of a number between one and ten, and every one of us guess the number, then whoever is closest wins."

The friends agree that's a good idea and call Rymer's dad on the walkie-talkie. They explain their idea when he comes out of the house and climbs up into the treehouse. They tell him to pick a number between one and ten. He thinks of it and says, "Okay, I got my number."

Rymer picks three. Ollie picks seven. Ash picks two. Nia picks ten.

Rymer's dad says, "My number was six, so, Ollie, you win."

Ollie says, "Okay, I pick an Xbox. I heard they have a sale going on at the store in town." He turns to Rymer's dad and says, "Mr. Strauss, can you tell us how much it will be to buy an Xbox?"

"No problem," he says with a chuckle. "I actually just bought one for Rymer's brothers. We bought an Xbox Series X for $699, and that came with two games and two controllers."

"We might want to get extra headsets. I think those are around twenty dollars each," says Rymer.

"And don't forget the TV!" says Ash. "How much is a TV?"

Rymer's dad pulls his phone out and, after a moment, says, "You can get a forty-two-inch TV for $549. So if you add that all up, assuming you get two extra controllers and taxes, that's ..." He punches his phone a few times. "Just about $1,400."

Ash blows all the air out of his lungs. "That's so much money!"

Rymer's dad chuckles again and says, "It sure is. Being a grown-up is hard. It gets old fast! Get it? Gets old?"

"We got it, Dad," Rymer says, and the kids all roll their eyes.

Rymer's dad climbs down from the treehouse and walks back to the house, still laughing a little at himself.

Rymer puts the friends back on topic, saying, "Okay, now that we know what to buy and how much it costs, how do we get the teeth out?"

Nia says, "Like Rymer said before, we could always do it the old-fashioned way by tying the tooth to a door, then slamming it."

Ash says, "I'm good to do that as long as it's not me being tied to the door."

Nia volunteers this time, so the gang sets everything up, and Ollie slams the door with a bang! And Nia's head gets yanked forward. "Ouch!" she cries.

She pulls the string off her tooth and starts to pull on her tooth with her fingers. Ash face-palms and says, "Nia, you know that's not going to work, right?"

But Nia smiles. The kids see a little blood in her mouth, and there, in between her fingers, is one of her front teeth. "It was loose anyway!" she exclaims, holding it out for them to see.

"How much do you get from the tooth fairy?" asks Ash.

"I get eight dollars," she says proudly.

Rymer gets her some tissues for her bloody tooth and says, "Eight dollars? I get twelve dollars. How much do you guys get?"

Ollie gets six dollars. Ash gets five dollars and a box of Cheerios.

"How many teeth do we have anyway?" Rymer asks.

The kids all stick their fingers in their mouths and start counting. They realize that they each have only twenty baby teeth. He gives each kid a marker and tells them to do the math to figure out how much money they will each get if they lose all their teeth.

Nia multiplies eight times twenty and gets $160. Rymer multiplies his twelve and gets $240. Ollie gets $120. Ash gets $100 and a bunch of Cheerios.

They add it all up. "You guys," says Rymer, "we're only going to get $620. And it really hurts. I think it's time to call off Operation Baby Teeth."

"But I get to say I earned the first dollar! I'll bring it back in the morning," says Nia, carefully tucking her tooth in her pocket.

After a long day of hard work, they all head for home rubbing their sore cheeks.

CHAPTER 4

ALL HANDS ON DECK

The four of them meet up the next day at the treehouse to talk. "Well, that was a bust," Nia says, letting her tongue poke in and out of the new gap between her teeth. "But at least we made some money."

She pulls eight dollars out of her pocket and waves it in front of her. When they finished their treehouse, the four of them had hidden a Sonic the Hedgehog wallet inside the beanbag for all their future earnings. The zipper is underneath so it's easy to find but can't be seen from the outside. They think this is a very clever place to stash money; however, this is the first time something has been in it besides Ollie's stale gum.

They all have sore jaws and only eight dollars to show for it. If they ever want to see their awesome game set up before school starts, they are going to need a new plan. And fast.

Rymer grabs the markers and goes over to the Game Plan board. "No idea is a bad one," he says, turning to his friends for help. "Let's brainstorm!"

"I know a family down the block that has a lot of money," Ash says.

"How?" Rymer asks.

"Oh, they won the lottery." After a short pause, Ash adds, "Hey! That's it! We just need to buy a whole bunch of lottery tickets, and then we're bound to win. Bound to win!"

"One problem," Nia responds. "We only have eight dollars." She pulls the money out of her pocket and shows them. "And I'm not going to waste it on a lottery ticket."

"We need an idea that doesn't need money to begin with," Ollie says. "We're broke."

"What if we sell something?" Ash says. "Now, who has a lot of something that we could sell?"

"My sister has a ton of toys. Maybe we could convince her it was for a better cause," Rymer says. He writes "Sell Toys" on the Game Plan board.

"Even if you convinced her, your parents would freak," Nia says. "You know how adults are."

"True," Rymer says. "But what about our toys?"

"I kinda like my toys," Ollie says. The kids all think about their rooms that are full of all the things they love. No one wants to give up everything just to play video games.

"Okay," Ash says, "maybe not a lot of something but maybe something that we can sell for a lot of money."

"Well, my stepmom always says family is the most valuable thing," Rymer starts. "Hmmm ... What if we sell Molly?"

"Rymer!" everyone yells.

"Okay! Okay! I was just kidding. I would never do that. Molly is a good sister."

Just then, Nia sneezes loudly. "Gah! Pollen!" she says, sniffing and wiping the back of her hand across her nostrils.

Pollen. Rymer looks out the window at the driveway just in time to see his dad driving up. The top half of his car is covered in a fine layer of yellow dust.

"That's it!" Rymer says. "Pollen!"

"Pollen is never a good thing. And we can't sell it, if that's what you're thinking," Nia argues.

Rymer is too busy writing on the idea board to respond. He moves to the side, and the kids all read it out loud: "Car Wash!"

"Listen," Rymer says. "Both my dad and stepmom have really nice cars that can only be hand-washed. My stepmom's is really cool because it has a ladder on the back of it that is fun to climb on and see the world from the top of the car. Plus, look at how much pollen there is on my dad's car. Every car is especially dirty this time of year. And the car wash is really far away."

"Yeah, and all that pollen makes my eyes watery and itchy," Nia adds with a sniffle.

Ollie sighs and says, "Come on, guys. What kid has ever owned a car wash business?"

Ash gets a big, goofy grin. "We are cute! The adults will come running."

Rymer laughs and adds, "And we have lots of energy, so we can wash a bunch of cars. And fast. I watch my dad wash his car all the time, so I know exactly what to do. It's easy. Just soap and water, right?"

"Hey, that might actually work," Ollie says, getting up and taking the marker from Rymer. He writes "What We Need" underneath "Car Wash."

"We need soap, washcloths, and buckets of water. Maybe some sponges," he says as he adds them to the Game Plan board.

Ash takes charge. "Sure. I'll bet we can find all that stuff in our houses. But first, we'll need a good name. Something to put on a sign. To put on a sign."

"How about Soap and Slide?" Ollie asks.

"Samurai Suds!" Nia blurts out.

"Buds with Suds," Rymer says.

"I like Super Suds Wash," Ash adds.

"No, no. I think it should be All Hands On Deck Car Wash," Ollie says, pumping his hands up and down like he is on a game show. "We live on an island, and there are tons of boats everywhere, and sailors say 'all hands on deck' all the time! What do you think?"

The other three agree, and Ash says he has a bunch of poster boards at his house that they can use for the signs. They grab the markers and head over to his house.

"So where are we going to do this car wash anyway?" Nia asks as they walk.

"We could start in each of our driveways and do our parents' cars," says Ollie.

Ash suggests, "Have you seen all the pollen on the cars around the neighborhood? We could be a delivery service for car washes. Like if we were delivering pizza to them but instead it's a car wash."

Nia asks, "How are we gonna carry all those supplies with us? That will never work. Have you ever had to haul a bucket of water? I use them in my training sometimes. They are heavy!"

Rymer suggests, "We could haul everything on that red wagon in Ollie's garage."

Nia asks, "What if we run out of supplies, and we are really far away from our houses? This neighborhood is really big with hundreds of homes on over a dozen streets. How about this? Let's go to the big marina in the middle of the bay. That has lots of boats. We could wash boats and cars."

"Boats are already in the water, Nia. In the water. They don't need to be washed. They just get splashed when they're out doing boat stuff in the ocean," says Ash.

"How about at the school parking lot?" Ollie suggests.

"Who is going to drive to the school in July? No cars there," Rymer says.

"How about the side of the highway?" Nia says. "There's always lots of cars there."

"Nope," Ash says. "The cars can't stop on the highway. I think it's a law or something."

"How about the park?" Rymer asks.

"That's over a mile away!" Ollie explains. "We can't haul all this stuff that far!"

"The beach?" Ash asks.

"Yeah!" Ollie replies. "At the beach, there are lots of people, places to pull over, and it's not illegal to stop!"

"But it's mostly tourists who go to the beach, guys. They rent cars, so they don't have to clean them," Nia says. "They aren't going to need to wash a car they don't own."

"Where else is there?" Ash asks, getting frustrated.

"Our houses, like I said already," Ollie grumbles.

"Wait! That's it! Ash, you live in a circle!"

"Yeah. There are like six houses on the same circle. They will all see how good of a job we do and will probably hire us."

"And it's safe for cars to pull over. Plus, it's not too far away. I vote that!" Nia says. Everyone agrees just as they get to Ash's house.

After a few hours of coloring, they stand back to look at what they've made. The signs are super big, so that's good. They all say

"All Hands On Deck Car Wash," but they are all in different colors because there weren't enough markers to use the same color for all the letters. Plus, Ash kept adding stuff to everyone's signs like, "We are really good at washing cars!" and "We are just kids!" and even "Help us!" They might not look the best, but the kids think they will get the attention of the grown-ups who drive by.

The kids decide to leave all their posters in the treehouse, agreeing to come back in the morning to start getting their supplies together.

The next day, they are back in the treehouse. Ash stands at the Game Plan board, pointing to his list. "Okay, guys. We need to figure out how to get all this stuff. I don't think any of our parents are going to just give us the chemicals. Mine will barely even let me open the fridge. The fridge! I think we need to figure out how to get them without anyone noticing."

Rymer gets an idea. "My parents have all kinds of supplies so they can hand-wash their really cool cars. We just need to sneak into the garage and grab the cleaning stuff before anyone notices. Easy!"

Even though they were barely settled into the treehouse, they all turn around and climb back down. They send Ollie to get his red wagon, and the rest of them head for Rymer's garage, crouching down and creeping like bandits in the night. They silently open the garage door and go to a cabinet. Rymer whispers as he opens it, "Everyone, take one of everything."

They snatch the buckets, soap, sponges, rags, and everything else that they think might be useful for their car wash. Their arms are full when Nia stops.

"Why do you have so much stuff for washing cars?" she whispers, stuffing sponges in a bucket.

"Oh yeah! My brother did a car wash as a fundraiser for his soccer team. We even have his old sign!" Rymer pulls out a white sign with blue font that says, "Support the Sunfish. Get your car washed today!"

"Do we have everything?" he asks, putting the sign back.

Just then, Ollie bangs open the garage door. "I have the wagon!" he yells, his voice echoing in the big garage.

Everyone freezes for a moment, then they turn to him and say, "Shh!" They motion him over, and he pulls the wagon through the door as carefully as he can. They all listen to see if anyone is coming, but when nothing happens, they relax.

"Do we have everything?" Rymer whispers again.

"Um, I don't have a sponge. Or soap," Ollie says as quiet as Ollie can be—which isn't actually that quiet.

"You can share with me. With me," Ash whispers back, putting his arm around Ollie.

"That won't work," Nia says, her voice getting a little louder.

"Why not?" Ash says. "We love sharing."

"I'm with Ollie on this one," Rymer says. "We can clean quicker if we are not sharing a sponge. I guess we have to go find another sponge. Oh, and more soap. You guys stay here."

He creeps through the living room, and he sees Molly playing with her Barbies on the rug. She gives Rymer a puzzled look. He straightens up and goes into the kitchen, where he grabs the soap and sponge and walks back into the garage. As he closes the door, Molly finds their dad and tells him what she saw.

Rymer's dad doesn't think they are stealing anything, but he is definitely concerned that they are going to make a slip-and-slide or make a giant mess in the backyard. He has a feeling they are doing something they shouldn't. Of course, by the time he gets his shoes on and goes down to the garage, the kids are gone and so are the supplies. He sees that the cabinet they left open is empty. He checks the treehouse, but they aren't there.

The four of them are walking down the street toward Ash's house. Rymer's dad immediately calls Ollie's dad because he knows if Rymer is up to something, Ollie is up to something. And if Ollie is up to something, Ash is up to something. And if the three boys are up to something, then, of course, Nia is up to something.

Ollie's dad hasn't seen the kids, and they can't get in touch with Ash's or Nia's parents. He suggests they go to Ash's house to see if the kids are there. Before they hang up, Ollie's dad says, "If they are not there, I'm sure we will find them on the way."

CHAPTER 5

A GRAND SCHEME GOES DOWN THE DRAIN

Just as the kids get to Ash's driveway and begin taking the supplies out of the wagon, two cars come speeding down the road and head straight for them.

"Wow!" says Ollie. "Word spreads fast. Looks like we have our first two customers already."

"Cool! Everyone, smile and wave. That way, they'll know they are in the right place," Rymer says. They put everything down and wave their hands, big grins on their faces, and Ash holds the sign up over his head.

"Wait. Isn't that your car, Rymer? And yours, Ash?" Nia says, dropping her hands in disappointment.

Just as she says that, Rymer's dad opens the car door and steps out. He doesn't look too happy. Neither do Ollie's mom and dad as they both step out. Then out tumble Ollie's little brother, John, and little sister, Millie. They run over to the wagon and climb in with all the cleaning stuff. Molly gets out last, looking a little hurt that she got left behind.

"What are you kids doing here? And what is all of this?" asks Ollie's mom, taking a sponge out of Ollie's brother's mouth.

The kids start talking at once, feeling nervous and excited all at the same time. They are worried that they might be in trouble, but they notice that their parents don't seem too mad.

"Okay," says Ollie's dad. "Let me get this straight. You're all trying to earn money by washing cars, is that right?"

"Yes! For an Xbox and a TV for the treehouse!" says Ollie.

"We're starting a company! Dad, I thought you said it was okay," says Rymer, holding up one of the signs.

"Peter," says Ollie's dad to Mr. Strauss, "are you okay with this?"

"Well, I knew they had the idea to get the gaming system. That's fine with me. But, kids," he says, turning to them with a stern look, "you really need to ask before you take things. You know that. From now on, please tell us what you are doing before you do it. We can help you. All you have to do is ask."

"Sorry, Dad," Rymer says. "I will talk to you about everything from now on."

"Me too," says Ollie. He picks up his little sister, who is wearing a rag on her head like a scarf. He laughs and says, "We could sure use some help. Can they stay and wash cars with us?"

"Me too!" says Molly. She picks up a sign and says, "I am really good at waving. I can get people to come here."

"That sounds okay to me," says Ollie's mom. "How are you going to keep track of all the money you make?"

Ash says, "How about we use a bucket? I have one in my room that is perfect for this!"

Ollie's mom says, "That sounds good, but first we need to know if your family is okay with you all being here. Ash, does your mom know what you're doing?"

Ash looks bashful. "No. I'll go get her."

He runs into the house and comes back with her after a couple of minutes. He uses sign language with her for a minute while everyone else watches. She signs back, and Ash says, "She says it's okay with her as long as we clean up after ourselves."

She smiles at them, points to the buckets and to the house, and signs to Ash again. He explains, "She says we can use the hose to run water from the house to fill up our buckets. And she wants us to dump the used water on the lawn so that it gets watered. No sense in wasting all the water on hot days like this."

The kids know how to sign "thank you" by touching their mouths with their fingers and reaching their hands out toward her. She smiles and signs "you're welcome" back by touching her thumb to her chest with her fingers stretched out and bouncing her hand a couple of times. Then she adds some more signs. Ash says, "Mom says it's getting a little late in the day for a car wash. She thinks it's a better idea to start in the morning."

The adults all look at their watches. The kids notice the sun is getting low in the sky. "Yeah, I think she's right," says Rymer. "Let's start after breakfast tomorrow. Does that work for everyone?"

They all agree and head home. Ash and his mom take the wagon full of supplies and the signs into their garage to save for the next day.

The next day, Rymer jumps out of bed excited. It's car wash day! He walks down the stairs and pours himself a bowl of cereal. When he finishes eating, he puts his bowl in the sink. Then he hears the walkie-talkie crackle. He forgot he had brought it inside and left it on the counter. Ollie says, "Rymer. Come in, Rymer. Meet at my house in thirty minutes. We'll go to Ash's house together. Over."

Rymer picks up the walkie-talkie and says, "Ten four. I'll be there with Molly. Over."

He walks upstairs to wake up Molly. He shakes her bed, and she wakes up with a grin on her face as she exclaims, "All hands on deck!"

Rymer makes Molly some cereal, and when she is done, they go to the backyard by sneaking through the secret passageway. They meet Ollie and walk to Ash's front yard. Ollie's little brother and sister are ready too. They all walk over together, noticing how many dirty cars there are on the streets. They are all excited about how much money they are going to make!

When they get there, Ash and Nia are already setting things up. They split the jobs up. Rymer is the street salesman along with Ollie, trying to steer traffic toward the car wash. They put the little kids in charge of the signs. "You guys need to help get people to notice us," Ollie explains.

The kids run around the sidewalks of the cul-de-sac, waving the signs in front of each house and yelling out things like "Car wash!"

"Best car wash ever!"

"Get your car clean!"

"All hands on deck!"

And for some reason, John starts yelling, "Aye, aye, captain!" over and over again.

Sam, Matt, and Isabelle are walking down the street. Rymer walks over to them and says, "Do you want to join us in our car wash business?"

All three of them say "Yes!" at the same time as they walk back over to the car wash station.

After about thirty minutes, a car pulls up. Their first customer is a neighborhood security guard named Bobby who was driving by and saw all the commotion. He's a big guy with a massive belly and not much hair on his head. He's really nice, and before he knows what is happening, the kids have swarmed. They are climbing all over his car and hosing it down and spraying the windows and dripping soap all over. Bobby just rolls with it.

Bobby is younger than the kids' dads, but he is not a teenager, Rymer figures as he looks through the soapy window. His car was actually pretty clean already. He keeps it that way because he's important in the neighborhood and wants to keep things nice for everyone.

After all the chaos calms down, he rolls down the window and hands the kids ten bucks, which they think is a total score.

The next customer is a big truck, which is much harder because it is not low to the ground at all. The customer rolls down his window and says, "Best car wash, huh? It says that on your sign. Let's test this theory. How much is this 'best car wash' of yours?"

Ash looks at Rymer. "Oh, shoot! We forgot to come up with a price, didn't we?"

Rymer replies, "Oops! Yes, we did." He takes a deep breath and looks at the customer. "It seems as though we forgot to come up with a price, sir. You can just give us what you think is fair."

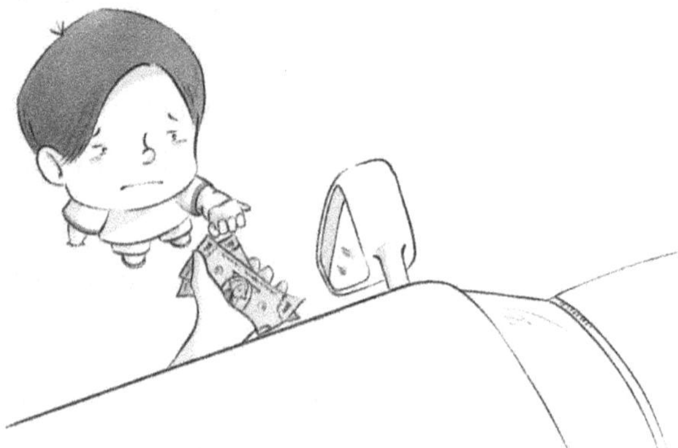

The guy hands him three one-dollar bills, and Rymer tries to hide his disappointment. The kids start working. Ollie is back to sign flipping, trying not let his discouragement show. Ash is helping Ollie's sister wash the car, and Nia and John are getting ready to dry with some rags. Midway through washing, Ash notices that none of them can reach the top of the car, and it's the dirtiest part of the truck.

Ollie looks at Matt and says, "Can you reach the top of the car?"

Matt says, "I can try." He does as much as he can and gets most of it, but he misses a little bit that is in the middle. They look at Molly, who is taller than Millie, and they get an idea.

They ask Molly if she wants to climb onto Matt's shoulders. Of course Molly accepts, but she can't really wash the top because she is too busy trying to keep balanced. She won't let go of Matt's ears, so he gives up. Finally, Nia climbs on Matt's shoulders, and they reach the last part of the truck. The customer drives off happy.

Then a bigger truck comes up. To get to the top of it, Rymer and Nia try to make a human pyramid and tell Ash to climb on top. That works for a second, but it ends up with all three of them on the ground.

They decide to form another pyramid with all the big kids on the bottom and all the little kids on top of them. It sort of works, but the kids are too busy giggling to do any washing.

Molly tries to climb on top of the truck, but the customer opens his window and yells, "Don't dent my truck!"

Finally, Rymer tells the driver, "I'm sorry, but we couldn't get the top of your car. We are just too short."

The driver grumbles and drives away without paying them. The next car pulls in, and Rymer sighs. He whispers to himself, "It's gonna be a long day."

This time, it's a sports car, which is much easier because it is lower to the ground. The group has little trouble with this car and gets paid ten dollars. A few more cars come and go while Rymer looks in the money bucket, seeing how little money is in there. Nia suggests that they should go find people who drive golf carts because they are really popular and easier to clean. None of the other kids like this idea because they think they can't charge good money for a golf cart.

At one point, Rymer tries to charge everyone a hundred dollars, thinking that way they would only have to wash ten or fifteen of them. But nobody will pay that much. The drivers all laugh at the suggestion.

For the rest of the day, they don't really charge anyone anything since they don't know what to charge anyway. Instead, they take whatever people give them. When people ask how much it is, they say things like "How 'bout five bucks?" or "How much do you want to pay?"

They get answers that range from "Okay" to "Can I pay you later?" to "Sure, but how about we pay after we see how good you guys do?"

They do a really good job on one car, and the nice old lady actually gives them seventy-five dollars!

They all work together. Nia is directing traffic. Ash tells the little kids where to spray the cars. Molly is trying to soap up the tires, but she ends up soaking her shoes instead and spends more time squishing bubbles out of her shoes and giggling than actually washing anything. They have given up reaching the roofs of the taller cars, so, depending on the type of vehicle, some of them are clean only up to the top of the windows since they try to reach the tops of cars without getting themselves soaking wet.

When not directing traffic, they have fun squishing bubbles, spraying each other, and throwing wet, soapy towels at each other. When they get thirsty, they just drink from the water hose.

It starts to get really hot and feels like it's already dinner time, but it is only 10:15 a.m.! A lot of time passes, and not a single car pulls over. Rymer is getting bored of holding the sign. Ollie gets tired of being enthusiastic and trying to attract customers with his okay-at-best sign flipping. Ash starts to play tag with the other kids, and Nia sits down and starts trying to slit blades of grass with her swords.

By the end of the day, the kids are ready to go home. As they clean up the mess, they try to figure out how many cars they washed. There is a lot of confusion. They think it is somewhere between twelve and seventeen, but they can't be sure. Nobody was in charge of counting the cars, so some got counted twice, and some were never counted at all.

"Oh well," says Rymer. "It doesn't matter. We made a little money anyway. We can count it in the treehouse in the morning. See you all tomorrow."

Everyone says their goodbyes and leaves. When Rymer and Molly get home, Molly plops down on the couch and tells everyone about the hard work she did. Rymer rolls his eyes and says, "You know that I was doing the same work as you."

Molly replies, "Yeah, but it still feels good to complaaain."

Rymer puts his face to his palm and shakes his head. Kristi walks over to the kids and says, "Hey, do you guys want to have a movie night tonight?"

They both agree and settle in to watch a movie with popcorn and soda pop. Not even twenty minutes into the show, Molly falls asleep. Kristi comments, "Wow, she really was tired!"

Rymer laughs and drifts off to sleep too.

CHAPTER 6

BUSINESS TYCOON

It's a lazy afternoon, and the kids are hanging out in their treehouse, passing the time on another hot and muggy summer day. After counting their money from the car wash disaster, they stash it in their Sonic the Hedgehog wallet inside the beanbag. They realize they have $223, plus Nia's $8, so that's $231.

Ollie has brought his calculator to use. It's actually part of a spy kit that he got for Christmas the year before. It came with invisible ink and paper to write secret messages on, X-ray glasses to see people without their clothes on (that for some reason never work), and this calculator that was supposed to attach to some plastic weapon that shot sticky stuff but was always jammed up. He just kept the calculator because it is really fun to count all kinds of stuff like allowance money, how many days till the end of school, how many birthday presents he was going to get to open, etc.

He uses his calculator to figure out that they still need $1,169. It might as well be a million dollars. They write it on the Game Plan board.

Ash is playing around with his remote control car. Ollie is reading a comic book, and Nia is doing sit-ups. Rymer is playing a video game on his brother Steve's phone, which he snuck out of the house after breakfast.

Only the hum of insects and the distant engine of a lawn mower can be heard until Rymer jumps up and shouts, "Yes!"

Ollie puts down his book and asks, "What?"

"My businesses just hit a million dollars in annual profit!" Rymer shouts, doing a little celebration dance.

"So what? I just did a million sit-ups," Nia says, breathing out a bored sigh.

"Really?" Ash asks, raising an eyebrow. "A million?"

"Well, I think so anyway. I kinda lost count after twenty. You get in the zone when you're training," she answers.

"Have you heard of the game Business Tycoon?" Rymer asks. "It's super cool. It's all about managing processes and profit margins and …"

"In English, Rymer! You sound like your dad," Ollie says.

"Okay. You start with one store and no employees, and you have to earn everything on your own until you make enough money to hire one worker. And then you keep making money and you have to buy stuff and sell stuff. Then you have to manage products and people so that you can open another store. And it goes on and on."

He looks at them and notices that they are all looking confused. "Okay, let's think of it this way. Do you all make an allowance?"

Nia and Ollie nod their heads, but Ash doesn't. He says, "I get money for my birthday and Christmas sometimes. Does that count?"

"Sure. Nia and Ollie, do you have to earn your allowance? I know I do. I have to take out the garbage and clean the leaves out of the pool. What do you guys have to do?"

Ollie has to clean his room and help with the dishes. Nia has to feed and water her dog and clean up after it. She also has to help her grandma fold laundry.

"Great" says Rymer. He continues, saying, "I get ten bucks as my allowance. Sometimes I pay Molly two dollars to take out the trash. See, I get ten dollars, spend two dollars on Molly—my employee. And while she takes out the trash, I count my money. Just imagine if I could get more jobs like mowing the lawn when I get bigger … my parents would pay me even more. Actually, I bet I could get them to pay me ten dollars for the lawn alone. Then, I can hire one of my brothers to do it for five dollars. Then I'd be making twenty dollars a week with two employees. They would earn seven dollars for doing the two things I don't want to do, and I get to keep the other thirteen dollars and think of other jobs I can hire people to do for me!"

Ollie has been clicking away on his calculator the whole time. "That makes sense to me."

Rymer says, "In the game, I have five stores and twenty employees, and it only took me two months to hit a million."

"Man, I wish we could figure something like that out for us in real life," sighs Ollie.

"Why not?" asks Rymer. "We can totally come up with a business plan. It's just a matter of knowing how to make a profit! I think we could each go home and ask our parents if there are any jobs we can do to get paid extra money. But then we can hire other people to do the actual work! There are tons of little kids in the neighborhood we can hire cheap."

The kids are a bit skeptical. Hiring cheap kids off the street seems a little sketchy. But in the end, they are up to trying it out since Rymer thinks it's a good idea. They make a pact that they won't do the work themselves; they will hire a friend or sibling to do it and report back in a while.

Ollie grabs a marker and writes "Operation Cheap Labor??" on the Game Plan board. All the kids start talking about boring jobs or not-so-fun jobs they have to do around the house. They get excited thinking about having someone else do the work for them while they sit back and count their money!

Just as they are leaving to go to their homes, a yell comes from the house. "Rymer! My phone!"

It's Steven, and he's still yelling. "I know you stole it to play my money game. Give it back, you little—"

Rymer's eyes get big, and he says, "We better go!"

They scatter. Ollie goes down the zipline. Nia grabs the sides of the ladder with her hands and feet and slips down without touching any of the rungs. Rymer goes down the slide, and Ash climbs down the ladder. Everyone except Rymer heads toward the secret passageway in the bushes to Ollie's house. Because of the humidity, the slide isn't very slippery, so he has to scoot down using his feet. Steve grabs him by the shoulders when he gets to the bottom. "Give it to me," he snarls.

Rymer says, "You never play that game anyway. But fine. Here!" He throws it in the air, and Steve lets him go so he can catch it. Rymer runs to the passageway and joins his buddies on the other side in Ollie's backyard.

After they all catch their breath, Ash says, "Are we still going to build our backyard business using our family as our employees?"

Everyone nods.

"Great," says Ash. "Should we meet back at the treehouse in one hour? One hour?"

They agree and go their separate ways.

CHAPTER 7

GOING FISHING

When he gets inside, Rymer checks to see if his brother is still mad, and when he can't see him, he goes downstairs to his dad's office. "Dad, how much would you pay me to mow the lawn?"

"Rymer, you are not old enough to mow the lawn. It is very dangerous."

"What about Steve and Branson? Are they big enough?" Rymer asks.

"Yes, but good luck getting them to help you out," his dad responds.

"Okay then, Dad. How about ten dollars to mow the lawn?"

Rymer's dad laughs and says, "If you can get your brothers to mow the lawn for ten dollars, that's a deal. Heck, I'd give you twenty dollars if you could get your brothers to do it."

He laughs again, but Rymer doesn't get it.

Ecstatic, he runs upstairs to where his brothers are, of course, gaming. He asks them, "Who wants to make ten dollars?"

They both put down their controllers, mildly interested. Rymer says, "All you gotta do is mow the lawn!"

They both break out laughing. "Dad would have paid us twenty-five. Why would we do it for ten?"

Deflated, Rymer realizes he can't talk his big brothers into doing anything at a discount like he can with Molly. He gives up and goes back to the treehouse to pout for the rest of the hour.

When his friends come back up to the treehouse, all of them have had similar experiences and take turns telling about their failures.

Nia says, "I asked my mom how much she would pay for some freshly baked cookies. She said she would pay five dollars for a dozen. I knew my grandma would make them for me for free if I asked nicely, and I was right. But every time I went to check on her in the kitchen, she had forgotten what she was doing."

Ollie had tried to convince his sister Millie to do the dishes for him, but she was on her way to ballet practice. He had gone to Anthony, his big brother, but when he had asked, "Would you like to do the dishes for me if I paid you?" Anthony had only heard "do the dishes" and gladly handed Ollie a stack of dirty bowls and spoons that had piled up on his desk.

Ash had tried to grab his little brother and sister and sit them down so he could tell them how great a deal he had for them. But they were too full of energy because their mom had accidentally left an energy drink on the counter, and they had just helped themselves to the rest of it. After an hour of trying to get them to listen, he was so tired that he gave up. Ash says with a sigh, "I finally understand why my parents are always so excited for bedtime. Getting those two to sit still is quite a job!"

While his trial at home failed, Ash's parents had asked him what he was doing. When they found out, they told him the country club that they play golf at always has kids selling golf balls that have been hit into the pond. They have long sticks with little ball retrievers on the ends, and they fish out the golf balls and sell them for a discount of one dollar a ball. And there are a lot!

Ash says, "Who would think you could make money on a golf course? On a golf course! I wonder what else we could sell at that place?"

Rymer jumps up and says, "That's it!" He grabs a marker and writes "The Great Lost Golf Ball Plan" on the Game Plan board. "We just need to go get a bunch of balls out of the water and sell them! Easy!"

"Before we have another money fail," Nia says, "let's figure out exactly how much we need and how much we have. That way we can have a goal that we know."

Ollie pulls out his handy dandy calculator and totals up the numbers that Rymer's dad had written down for them when they first had the idea. They need $1,400 minus the $231 they have, which equals $1,169 they still need. 1,400 – 231 = 1,169.

"If we collect the balls and nobody charges us anything, it's pure profit!" Rymer says. "We just need to collect 1,169 golf balls."

Nia says, "How hard could that be? Let's go down to the golf course and check it out."

The kids walk over to the neighborhood golf course, which is just behind Nia's house.

By this time, the day has gotten really hot, and they have to keep wiping sweat off their foreheads. There are hardly any other people there, which is good because they aren't really supposed to be out here. Nia learned this the hard way when she was younger and used to run around the course for her ninja training. She always got yelled at by the manager when he caught her.

But because she grew up here, she knows where all the equipment is kept. "I've seen them fishing balls out of the ponds sometimes using these big net things on poles. I even know where they keep them. Follow me!"

Nia leads them to a shed that is behind a bunch of golf carts. Thankfully the doors are open and there is nobody around. "Time for me to be like a ninja because if the manager catches us, we're toast. You guys wait behind there," Nia says, pointing to some bushes.

She sneaks into the shed, and after a couple of minutes, she comes out holding a long pole. They all take off running over a little hill where they are pretty sure nobody can see them.

"Where do we get the balls?" Rymer asks.

"Right there," Nia says, pointing to a small moon-shaped pond. They all run over to it. As they look over it, they realize they can't see very far out into the water. It's too muddy.

Ash scratches his head. "I guess we just have to drag this thing along the bottom and see what we get, huh?"

It's really heavy, so it takes all four of them to take a swipe near the edge, and sure enough, the net comes out of the water with a golf ball. They cheer and try it again. They are able to get a ball or two with every few swipes, but after a few minutes, they have been around the edge of the whole pond.

"How many do we have?" Rymer asks.

"Thirty!" answers Nia, who is collecting them in a sandy place on the ground, so they don't roll away. They are worth thirty dollars!

Ash wipes the sweat out of his eyes and says, "Let's try to get it really out there. I would guess all the balls are in the middle where it's deepest."

They all take hold of the rod and start pushing it forward into the water, but the farther out it goes, the heavier it seems. "Why don't you just go out and get them?" asks Nia to the boys.

"No way! There are fish in that water, and I don't want them to bite me!" replies Ollie.

"I'd do it, but Mom would kill me if I got my new shorts all muddy," says Ash.

Rymer adds, "I don't swim in water that I can't see through. No way."

"Fine," says Nia. "Let's just get it out really far then and see what we can get."

They push it out as far as they can, but because they are keeping it close to the ground, the net isn't getting deep enough. They try raising it over their heads, which is really hard because the higher they raise it, the heavier it gets. Suddenly, it slips out of their hands and sinks to the bottom of the pond, never to be seen again.

"Back to the drawing board," says Rymer.

Just then, the manager comes over the hill and yells, "Hey, kids. Get off the course! You aren't supposed to be here."

They all start running away, avoiding the mean manager. When they get close to the clubhouse, they slow down and talk about what just happened. They realize they didn't think about how to carry thirty golf balls, so they hope when they come back, nobody will have taken them. Of course, they all forget that there are a whole lot of golfers on the course who are happy to help themselves to a bunch of free balls in a convenient pile. The balls are all taken before the kids make it home.

As the kids walk off the course, they realize how thirsty they are. Ash says, "Boy, wouldn't a cold glass of lemonade be good right now?"

Ollie says, "Yeah. And I even have some change in my pocket right now. I wonder why they never have lemonade in vending machines."

"Hey, that's it!" Rymer yells a little too loudly. "Maybe we should be a vending machine!"

"I don't get it, Rymes. We're humans," says Ash.

"No, I mean maybe we should make lemonade and sell it to golfers on hot days … or just anyone who is thirsty!"

It dawns on them. Instead of fishing golf balls out of the lake to sell them, they could make lemonade and sell that!

CHAPTER 8

OH, SUGAR!

The next day, they are back in the treehouse, and a new label is on the Game Plan board: "Lemonade Stand." Rymer wrote it in big, yellow letters that morning and even drew a few lemons around it. Well, he tried at least. They kind of look like smudgy yellow footballs, but nobody seems to care.

"First things first," Rymer says. "We've got to make sure people know about our stand. We need some good signs, but let's not spend any money if we can help it. What can we use?"

"I know!" says Ollie. "There is a bunch of construction stuff by that new house. You know, the one that is getting built on the other side of our street. Let's go over there and see what we can find."

The kids run across the street and find a bunch of wooden pallets by the dumpster. But as they try to lift them up to take them to the treehouse, they quickly discover that the pallets are too heavy to lift. Besides, the pile of pallets is so big that there are a bunch of other kids playing on it. They don't want to wreck the playground. In fact, it seems pretty fun! So they join in.

After playing with everyone else for an hour or so, the four friends sit down under a nearby tree to think of a new plan. They love the idea of big signs and being able to walk and advertise at the same time, but they need something much lighter.

"I keep a ton of cardboard and posterboards in my playroom so I can draw up new targets to practice sword fighting and battle planning. Why don't we just use those?" says Nia.

"Yes!" the boys all say at once, and they all bike/run/scooter over to her house and settle into her playroom. While they start making the signs, Ollie asks, "Do any of you know how to make lemonade?"

Silence.

"Okay," says Rymer. "Maybe we need to do a little research. Nia, do you think we can use your parents' iPad to look up recipes?"

"Sure!" Nia leaves to ask her mom, and when she gets back, she searches "world's greatest lemonade" and finds a recipe with sugar, water, ice, lemons, and mint! The gang agrees that this is the recipe they should use—at least for now. They also notice that the recipe is rather vague, so they decide that they should use fresh-squeezed lemons, tap water, ice from the freezer, and mint picked from Ollie's brother's herb garden. But they don't know what type of sugar to use.

Ash says, "I like the sugar that my mom sprinkles on my waffles. The light, fluffy stuff."

Rymer says, "I like brown sugar in my oatmeal. That would probably be good in lemonade."

Ollie thinks for a minute and then says, "I heard honey is healthier than sugar. Maybe we should use that?"

They decide to figure it out later and finish the signs first.

When they are done, the gang goes back to Rymer's house because Rymer has a lemon tree in his backyard, and they figure they should pick a few. But when they get inside, they hear Molly upstairs.

"Hey, guys," says Rymer. "Molly is actually a sugar expert. She's always making cakes, brownies, cupcakes, cookies, magic potions, and on and on with Kristi, our stepmom. Let's ask her."

Molly is so excited to be the expert. She tells them that white granulated sugar works for baking and mixing drinks, but powdered sugar only works on top of things like pancakes and cupcakes. Then she explains the difference between real sugar and sugar substitutes and even other sweeteners like honey and molasses. "So you have to be careful to use the right stuff," she says as she finishes her lecture. "Or you'll end up with really gross lemonade."

Ash leans over to Rymer and says, "I can't believe she's only six years old. She's so smart!"

They thank Molly for the lesson and decide that they are ready to try a few different mixtures. They need to test out their juicing skills and see if they can actually make lemonade. Kristi has all the ingredients they need in the kitchen and agrees to let them have everything for free for this experiment on the condition that they clean up the kitchen after they are done.

They ask her to call all the parents and have them come over for their "taste-off" surprise, and the adults all come. Even Nia's dog, Terrence, comes along. Ollie is usually less afraid of Terrence than he is of other dogs because he knows him, but Nia tries to keep Terrence close to her just so Ollie doesn't have to worry.

Each kid mixes up a batch of lemonade, and they serve it to the parents, who are blindfolded, to see which is the best.

Ollie forgets the sugar in his recipe, and Ash's mom nearly spits it out. Rymer uses brown sugar even though Molly told him not to, and it is pretty gross, just as she said. Nia doesn't take the lemon seeds out, so hers is chunky. And Ollie has way too much water.

To make matters worse, as the cups are sitting on the counter waiting to be tested, Molly says, "You guys better be careful not to leave the drinks too long in those paper cups or it will leak out of the bottom. If you ask me, Styrofoam is much better because the lemonade won't leak out and make a big sticky mess and get you in trouble. Plus it keeps it cool longer."

"I think I see exactly what she's talking about," says Nia. "Look, mine has only been sitting here for a few minutes, and the paper cup is starting to fall apart. Darn paper."

She is right. The water, mint, lemon juice, and ice are leaking all over the counter and running down the side of the kitchen island. Terrence is licking the floors. Rymer's parents don't look too happy.

They tell the kids to hurry and clean up the mess before Terrence licks it all up. Rymer is worried he will be punished for this.

After they are done cleaning, they don't really know what they want to do for the rest of the day, so they do what they always do: go up to the treehouse. After a few minutes, Rymer's dad comes out to talk to them.

"Guys, that was a good idea, but your execution wasn't very good. Would you agree?" he asks.

The kids nod their heads bashfully. Rymer asks, "Are we in trouble?"

"No," his dad says. "But it's clear you haven't got a plan."

Rymer brightens up. "In the game Business Tycoon, there is a part where you can come up with a business plan. Let's come up with one for our lemonade business."

The other three stand there still looking at him confused, so Rymer's dad says, "Okay. It's not that complicated. Think about it like a soccer game. You all play soccer. You know how you come up with plays sometimes? There is a field, two goals, and two teams with lots of players who play goalie, defense, midfield, and striker. You know there are boundaries and referees. And you know that whichever team scores the most goals wins. Following me so far?"

They nod.

He finds a blank spot on the Game Plan board and draws out an actual game plan to show the kids how moving a ball down a field as a team and scoring a goal works. "But instead of a ball, you will need to move the supplies starting with the source, which means wherever you get them, to the goal—which is the customers."

He pauses for them to nod their heads. "Business is like this. But for our lemonade game, the cul-de-sac is our field. Each cup of lemonade we sell is like a point for our team. Instead of offense and defense, the roles on our team are things like suppliers to help us get what we need, workers to help make the lemonade, marketers to bring crowds to buy the lemonade—and our goalie is someone who is good with numbers to keep count of our money."

"That's me!" Ollie says. "And I can keep track of how much everything costs when we buy our supplies."

Rymer's dad smiles and says, "That's right! If you wanted to do things in a very official way, you could do some research on the laws of the city for selling things. Maybe we could even do a field trip to city hall. That way you can avoid having any trouble with the law."

Rymer wrinkles his forehead. “Nah. Research is soooooo boring. We are kids! Who’s going to be mad at us? Dad, I know you’re a lawyer, but I don’t actually know what that means, you know.”

His dad laughs, ruffles Rymer’s hair, and leaves.

Nia says, “But you know what? It might not hurt to see what the weather is going to be like so we can plan our sale on the hottest day.”

Ash laughs. “Nia! We live on an island where it’s always hot and sunny. Hot and sunny! I think we can just take our chances.”

It’s clear the kids are all in on winging it, so that’s the end of that conversation. After a few minutes of silence, Ollie says, “But I am a little worried that other kids might get the same idea. We don’t want anyone to steal our business. Can we all agree to be super secret about it until it’s time to sell?”

They all agree.

“How could we lose?” says Ash.

Ollie nods his head. “Yeah. What could possibly go wrong?”

CHAPTER 9

START-UP FUNDS

The kids are so excited about their new idea that they keep brainstorming ideas even after Rymer's dad leaves the treehouse. They are all standing together in front of the Game Plan board because they are too excited to sit. There's so much to do, there is just no time to sit down! Molly comes up, and they tell her to stay because they need her help with ideas.

They decide they need a checklist to keep everything straight, so they add a new section on their board called "Stuff We Need." Under it they make a list: cups, pitcher, water, lemons, stirring spoon, money for change, money bucket, napkins, signs, ice.

"Don't forget sugar!" says Molly.

"I'm sure there will be more things we need, but this gets us started," says Rymer. "Ollie, can we keep using your wagon to carry the lemonade and signs and stuff to Ash's house?"

"I think so. I'll ask my mom when I get home," Ollie says. "But I want to talk about building the lemonade stand. What are we going to build it out of?"

"Remember those pallets at that new house across the street? I know they were too heavy to drag, but if we can lift them onto the wagon, we could get a couple of them into our garage," says Rymer. "Then we can use that wood to build it."

"But we haven't talked about jobs yet, you guys," says Nia. She starts counting off on her fingers as she says, "Someone has to make the lemonade, someone has to deliver it to the stand, someone has to sell it and collect money, someone has to run around and let everyone know the world's best lemonade is for sale ... and I don't think we want to use the money we have earned to get all the supplies. Remember Kristi told us we could have those supplies for free, but that was it. We are going to have to buy all the stuff to get started somehow."

"Oh yeah," says Ollie. "We're still kinda poor."

They all sit in silence for a few minutes, trying to figure out what to do next.

"I know!" says Ash. "My parents had a man come to our house a while ago and he had this big presentation about some great idea he had for a business. He had charts and graphs and a whole big speech, and when he was done, he asked them to be investors. I didn't know what they meant, but my dad told me it meant they would give him some money to get his business going. And when it was doing well, they would get the money back plus extra money for believing in him. Maybe we can do something like that? Find investors?"

Rymer gets a big smile on his face and says, "And we could have a big presentation here in the treehouse for them!" Rymer loves the idea of having guests in the treehouse and having the gang dress up all fancy and do a big performance to show the grown-ups why they should give them money.

He adds, "Let's have a top secret"—he uses air quotes—"meeting where we each invite one person we think would give us money."

The gang loves the idea, and everyone picks one person they want to invite. They spend the rest of the afternoon planning their super top secret business presentation, complete with invitations containing a ticket to get into the meeting. They are all so excited that they don't even notice the sun go down until Kristi calls for Rymer to come in for dinner. They all leave to go home, looking forward to the next day.

The kids find that their parents are all supportive of the meeting because they never get invited to the treehouse, and they always want to know what the kids are up to. The adults are told that they have to keep it a secret, though. If they tell anyone about it, they will have to deal with Nia, but they know the adults won't tell anyone.

The next day, the kids spend all morning preparing for their business meeting. They run back and forth between their homes and the treehouse gathering supplies and preparing. They gather a few snacks and sodas from their kitchens that their parents let them take up to the treehouse to prepare for the meeting.

At 4:00 p.m., they all go home to get dressed in their most businesslike clothes and comb their hair. Rymer even puts on a little of his dad's cologne, but when he walks past Molly, she says he stinks, so he washes it off.

At 5:00 p.m., their guests start to arrive. Ash and Rymer have both invited their dads, and Nia and Ollie have invited their moms. Nia waits on the ground to take their tickets, and she tells each adult that they have to climb up the rope ladder. As expected, they have trouble climbing it.

But they are good sports, taking turns one at a time. Once inside, they can't fit on the beanbag, and most of them end up sitting on the floor, which makes the room feel rather tiny once everyone is in. The kids think it is hilarious to watch all the adults try to get into the house, and the furniture (what little furniture they have) is all sized for kids, not adults, so they look folded up! They look like that circus act where a bunch of clowns try to fit into a tiny car.

They are all having so much fun getting to hang with the kids that they forget the small stuff and just play along.

Nia and Molly have carefully laid out the snacks and drinks, have cleaned up the place a bit, and have homemade flyers of "ROAR'N LEMONADE! WORLD'S BEST!" The papers are handed out with each of the parents' names on them.

In truth, the flyers are not really flyers. They are really just pictures drawn by Molly and Nia of a great-looking glass of lemonade on it, a stick figure representing each kid handing it to a parent, and a parent with a smiling face handing over a dollar.

The boys, on the other hand, have not contributed much at all to the setup of the meeting. They are messy, have markers and cardboard everywhere, and are so excited they can't sit still. Thankfully, they have the girls to keep everything in order.

They share their idea with the parents by taking turns showing their Game Plan board and explaining all the steps that they have taken to get to here. After they are through, they know it's time for the moment of truth.

Rymer was nominated to be the salesman of the meeting, so he takes a deep breath and says, "You can see that we need some money to buy the stuff we need." He points to their list. "How much would you be willing to invest in ROAR'N Lemonade? We will even pay you back with a little extra!"

After some discussion among the adults, the kids are told they can borrow "up to fifty bucks" with the understanding that someone will go with the kids to get the supplies.

"I know you kids," says Nia's mom with a laugh. "If someone doesn't watch you, you'll probably blow all the cash on junk."

Ollie proudly tells the grown-ups as they leave that they will be paid back "probably within the first hour because ROAR'N Lemonade is literally the best lemonade ever!"

After some more discussion among the adults, who are now gathered in Rymer's kitchen, Kristi agrees to be the designated assistant and take them the next day to the store to get what they need. Everyone else has to work, and she has the day off. Besides, she was planning to go shopping anyway, so it's not out of the way.

The next morning, the kids pile into her car and are so excited when they get to the grocery store she can't get them to stop running up and down the aisles and bringing back suggestions for things they may also need.

Rymer throws a candy bar into the cart. "It could be like a prize for the best customer!" he says.

"Or the best tipper!" says Ash.

"Come on, guys," Kristi says as she puts it back. "We need to stay focused on the lemonade."

For the next hour, Rymer's stepmom does her best to corral the kids and get through the shopping trip, and even though it is chaos, she can't help but laugh and take part in the fun. In the end, they spend $48.93 of Rymer's dad's investment, and Ollie keeps the receipt so he can add it to the paper where he is keeping track of their money. "We have to pay this back, don't forget," he reminds everyone on the way home. "Every penny counts."

When they get back to Rymer's house, the kids unload all the supplies they have purchased. They start making lemonade experiments to see what recipe they want to use.

Nia and Molly think it would be good to have pink lemonade, so they try everything from red apples to licorice to try to make it. In the end, they just add pink food coloring and extra sugar to make it sweeter. "Just like girls are sweeter than boys," says Molly.

Ash puts some hot sauce in a cup to try making spicy lemonade. He says, "Just to give it a kick." Rymer takes a sip and thinks he's going to die. Nope to the spicy lemonade idea.

But everything they make doesn't taste good enough to be the "world's best lemonade." After a few hours and a lot of mess, they all go home to ask their families to help them research recipes. In the end, Nia's grandmother is the hero. She introduces Nia to Samurai Sugar, a lemonade recipe from the family dynasty's early years. It is a recipe that has been passed down generation after generation. Because it is top secret, she only tells Nia the recipe as long as she gets as much free lemonade as she wants! Nia takes on the title of Lemonade Maker Boss Girl, and the boys are happy to let her.

They talk about what everyone else wants to do, and they decide that since Ollie is so good at math and has his trusty calculator all the time, he should be Money Man. Ash wants to be in charge of making sure their signs and everything look good, so they make him Sign Guy. Molly decides she wants to be the Cuteness Expert, who makes sure that everyone is smiling and acting happy for the customers. And Rymer wants to be the one who solves any problems that come up, so they all start calling him Head Problem Solver.

Just for fun, Rymer tells everyone to get in a circle and put their hands in the middle like he has seen his big brothers do before ball games. He likes what the coaches do, so he tries it out. "Everyone say 'ROAR'N' on the count of three. Ready? One. Two. Three …"

They fling their hands in the air and yell, "ROAR'N!" as loud as they can. They really are roaring and ready to go!

CHAPTER 10

LET'S JUICE!

It's time to start making their lemonade, and they know the first thing they want to do is get the lemons off the tree in Rymer's backyard. It seems like that would be more fun than just buying them at the store. Kristi tells them that they really need to make sure they have enough lemons before they get started so she can make a plan to run to the store to get more if they run out.

The kids try several ways to count the lemons. They each take turns counting what they see but keep losing count because the lemons don't grow in straight lines. They try spreading out and each counting sides of the tree, but because they are counting out loud, they all keep losing their place as they talk over each other.

Ollie decides the best way to count them is to climb the tree and count them as he throws them down to the others. The tree is pretty big but not very sturdy, so after a few attempts to climb the tree, they decide it may be better to make a human pyramid and then swat the lemons down. Those they can't reach can be knocked with a broomstick.

Nia is perfect for this job. She's the lightest of the group, samurai strong, and coordinated enough that she won't fall over. It works! And soon the kids are surrounded by lemons. They pull out the front of their T-shirts to load up the lemons and carry them inside.

They tell Kristi how many they have, and she decides that this isn't nearly enough. "I can trust you, can't I? You won't make a big mess while I'm gone to the store, right? I'll only be gone for half an hour, so I'm leaving Molly here with you."

"Of course!" says Rymer, fluttering his eyelashes as fast as he can. "We'll be little angels! Molly can even help us."

She laughs and grabs her purse before leaving, and Molly runs into the kitchen from the living room where she has been listening.

"Okay, guys," says Ash. "Let's get going! We need to get the juice out of all these lemons, but how?"

Ollie takes a lemon and tries stomping on it. The lemon shoots across the room, and he has to chase after it. Ash tries, and he has better luck smashing the lemon under his shoe, but it still just shoots juice all over the floor. "I don't think anyone wants to drink floor lemonade," he says as he tries to wipe up the mess with a paper towel.

Rymer takes one in his hands and tries to squeeze it in his hands, but he isn't strong enough to break the peel. Then he sticks it with a fork, and juice just dribbles out but not enough to fill even a small cup.

Finally, Nia has had enough watching the boys muscle the lemons without any success. She calmly gets a giant bowl and pulls a little lemon squeezer from the top drawer next to the sink.

"Duh," she says as the boys look at the giant mess they made on the floor and countertops. "I saw this here last time we were here. Didn't you know you had this, Rymer?"

"I've seen it, sure. But I didn't know that's what it was for," Rymer admits.

She slices a lemon in half with one of her swords and shows them how to squeeze each half. As they take turns slicing and squeezing, they start to wonder how much they should charge.

They all agree that it should be fifty cents for a cup of regular lemonade, seventy-five cents for pink lemonade, and a dollar for a cup of each.

Ash has the idea to charge two dollars for a refillable cup, like they do at the gas station. "People could get as much lemonade as they want, and we'll be able to make more money on them."

"What does 'unlimited' mean?" asks Molly.

"It means they can have as much as they want," explains Ash.

"But they can't really be unlimited," Rymer says. "That would mean we would be giving away a lot of free lemonade."

"Yeah," says Nia. "There has to be a maximum number of refills."

"Let's figure all that out later," says Ollie.

"Yeah, we'll just wing it," says Ash.

Rymer goes crazy. "No way, guys! Business is serious. We can't wing it, figure it out later, or give someone unlimited quantities. We won't have any profits!"

They all look at him, a little surprised at how passionate he is all of a sudden.

He goes on, calming down when he sees that he has their attention. "Two dollars for a refillable cup is a great idea but with a maximum of five cups. More than likely, nobody is going to drink five cups of lemonade."

"Yeah, right. They haven't tried my grandma's Samurai Sugar," says Nia. "I think it should be eight cups."

The kids are not sure who's right.

"Why don't you do rock, paper, scissors to decide?" says Ollie.

Nia and Rymer go to battle. Nia throws out a rock, and Rymer throws out a paper.

"Rymer wins!" yells Ash.

"Two out of three," says Molly. They agree. Nia throws a rock again, hoping to catch Rymer off guard. Rymer throws scissors.

"Nia wins!" yells Molly. Rymer is in disbelief, but he is determined. This time, he throws a rock, and Nia throws scissors. The boys start celebrating.

"Okay, it's final. Two dollars for a refillable cup up to five times," says Ollie.

Then Rymer stops. "Wait. What if the people we sell to only have bills? How are they going to pay fifty or seventy-five cents?"

"Well, that's easy," Ollie replies. "Let's see if we can use our parents' coin jars, and then we can just pay them back."

The kids know that their parents all have a ton of coins. Well, maybe not tons. But it looks like tons. The parents don't like carrying change, and so they take out whatever is in their pockets. Rymer's parents have a jar on their dresser. Ollie's have a bottle in the laundry room. Ash's keep a cup next to their keys in the kitchen. And Nia's family has a decorative bowl that is almost overflowing near their back door. They decide to ask their parents when they all get home that night.

After they finish juicing all the lemons, they put the pitcher full of lemon juice in the fridge and clean up their mess.

The group decides it's time to build the stand, so they go across the street to get the pallets and haul them in the wagon back to Rymer's garage. They struggle to get the pallets to stand up and stay next to each other to make a stand shape. The kids are not allowed to hammer things without an adult, and it's hard to nail things in as a fourth grader anyway.

Of all people, Molly suggests building the stand on top of the wagon. "Like a fort but on wheels so we can take it anywhere."

Rymer, not wanting his sister to steal the show, immediately chimes in, "Like when we put blankets on the couch and chair and use the pillows as weights. Then we get to hide under it."

Rymer's dad comes out to the garage and sees the kids putting together the mobile ROAR'N Lemonade stand and is blown away by their creativity. He walks back inside the house and has to admit to himself that the kids may have actually nailed it this time!

They work all afternoon, and when they are finally done, the display is awesome. It includes the wagon with pallets on the back, front, and on top. (Rymer's dad helped lift the top pallet and place it on the others. Then he helped nail everything in place.)

They take an old happy birthday tablecloth, flip it over, and place it on top of the wagon to make it look a little more fancy. Molly likes pulling the side of the sheet away from the wagon and clipping it onto the back of the chair with a clothespin she found to make a "tent." Then she crawls under it and hides. If it gets too hot, the kids can catch some homemade shade this way too.

They borrow a cooler from Ollie's family to keep ice in. There is a big glass jar that says "Tips" on it, and they have cardboard signs with strings on them so they can be worn around the neck, held up, or placed in front of the stand. There are a couple of treats for the kids hidden behind everything just in case they get hungry. Molly has graciously brought fidget toys for everyone and already seems to be too preoccupied playing with them to focus on lemonade sales.

They wheel the cart out of the garage so they can admire their work. The supplies are all lined up in pretty good order, but the napkins keep flying off the table.

"I know what to do!" Ash says. He digs into his pocket and pulls something out. "There. Problem solved!"

Ash has put his pet rock on top. It has the words "Pet Rock" written in permanent marker on it just in case someone asks.

CHAPTER 11

ROAR'N DAY ONE

The next morning is the big day! ROAR'N Lemonade will finally be open. It is a family affair with all the kids and their families there—even Rymer's two older brothers, who kind of want to see if Rymer can actually make money selling lemonade.

As the first hour goes on, most of the parents start to leave after agreeing the kids are safe and everything is all set up. It's pretty quiet for most of the morning. Every twenty minutes or so, one or two of the adults come by to casually check on them and watch the fun. They act like they don't notice the kids, but it's obvious to everyone that they are actually keeping an eye on things.

A jogger comes by with a dog, and he looks really hot. He's kind of big and sweaty and a little stinky.

"Just fifty cents, sir!" yells Ash as the jogger comes near. He stops running and pulls out his earbuds.

"How much for the pink one?" he asks.

Molly pokes her head out from under the table and says, "Seventy-five cents. And for just two dollars, you can—"

Rymer interrupts her. "We'll sell you a second glass for a dollar, and you can give it to your dog."

Molly frowns and says, "Why didn't you let me finish?"

Rymer pushes her head back under the table and whispers, "That guy can definitely drink more than five glasses, and I don't want to have to fight him."

The dog has been sniffing around in the street on a long leash until then, but it decides to come and check out all the kids.

Ollie freaks out when it comes by. He tries to hide under the table, but since Molly is under it already, he just backs way up. It's clear from the look on his face that he wants to run away, but he has a job to do, so he's trying to be brave.

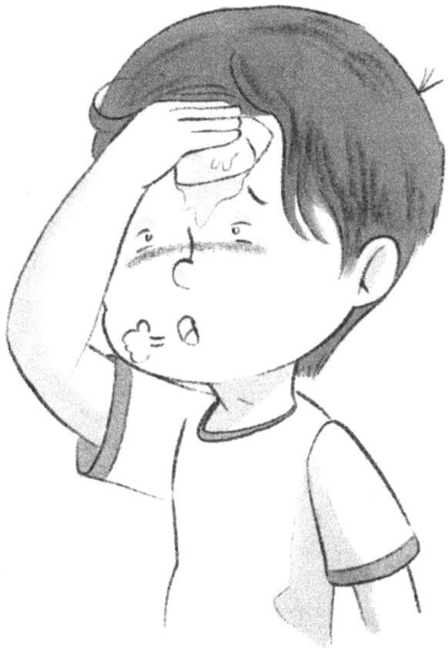

Rymer overhears Ollie's mom say to Rymer's dad, "I think maybe he has a crush on Nia. But I don't think he is quite sure what that means. At their age, girls are weird, right?" They laugh until they notice Rymer listening, so they move farther away.

The sweaty guy won't buy one for the dog, but he does leave a dollar tip—more than the lemonade costs. After that, Rymer's brothers leave when they realize that (1) yes, they can make money, (2) the younger kids are annoying and don't sit still, and (3) they would rather be inside where there is air-conditioning and electricity for their cell phones and video games.

The day continues to get hotter and windier, and the kids are struggling. Sam, Matt, and Isabelle have joined in the fun, but they are getting hot too. The spot under the table doesn't give that much shade, it's too cramped for more than one person, and it's boring in there because there is no one to talk to through a sheet. They take turns taking ice cubes from their cooler and running them across their foreheads and backs, but it's really cold on their backs and leaves them with wet shirts. And it uses too much of the ice they need for their sales.

They don't know what to do, but after a while, they decide they are too busy to worry about heat. They have a job to do. They are becoming business tycoons.

It feels like the entire neighborhood has come out for the lemonade sale. After the jogger, two ladies who were out walking see the super cute kids, the awesome wagon, and the delicious ROAR'N Lemonade. The ladies are amazed by the setup and comment on what hard workers they are. Of course, the kids don't tell them that Rymer's dad lifted and nailed all the pallets in place. Instead, Nia tells them she is strong enough to do everything herself.

As they start to walk away, other neighbors notice their ice-cold lemonade on this hot summer day, and nobody can miss the kids' very loud marketing pitches. As more customers come out, more kids come by to see what is going on. And they can't miss the cups and napkins that keep blowing off the table and down the street every time there is a breeze. Ash's pet rock just isn't heavy enough to hold much down.

Some of the kids are just curious; some want jobs when they realize money is being made. Molly is a real crowd draw because she starts handing out her fidgets to little old ladies because they always leave tips. Rymer starts a side hustle by offering great dad jokes for a quarter, and he gets a lot of tips. To be honest, he's not really sure if it is because he's got great jokes or because he's cute. Either way, he gets a lot of attention.

Ash looks around, leans over, and whispers to Nia and Ollie that they are going to be millionaires. "We are on fire! We could sell anything!"

They are so busy having fun and making money that they entirely forget lunch. Who needs lunch when you've got lemonade to sell? Besides, anytime they need something, one of the kids runs into Ash's house and gets it. They have to take turns because it's so hot out, and they all want to get some cold air.

Luckily for the kids, one of the early customers is Nia's grandma who always seems to think of everything. She is there, drinking one of her free cups of Samurai Sugar when a customer has a problem. She wants to buy many cups for a bunch of little kids that she has with her. She explains, "I'm a daycare worker, and we like to take the kids out for walks every day. But I didn't realize how hot it was going to be. And I never carry cash! Can I pay you electronically or with a credit card by any chance?"

"Just a moment. I think we can help you," Nia's grandma says. She immediately calls Rymer's dad with the issue. Knowing he was probably going to be needed throughout the day, he wasn't far. After all, he's got big bucks invested in the venture and wants to get paid back!

He has a chat with the customer, and before long, he tells the kids to pour as many cups as the woman wants. "Don't worry. She's going to pay me using her phone, and then I'll give you the money later."

The kids don't really know what it means to pay electronically, but since Rymer's dad promised they will get the money, they are okay with that. They find that many more customers want to pay that way as the day goes on, so they keep making and selling the lemonade until the sun starts to get low in the sky.

Finally, the day is over, and it feels like they've been working forever. "We're done!" Rymer sighs as he turns to the group.

"Come on, let's get everything cleaned up so everyone can go home," Ash's dad says as he comes out of the house.

Cleaning up is definitely *not* fun. The kids are all hot and tired, and they realize that there is lemonade, sugar, and melting ice all over. They keep licking their fingers, wrists, and arms because there is a weird sugar coating on everything.

Molly collapses on the ground and says dramatically, "My cheeks are sore from fake smiling, and I'm too sticky!"

Nia says, "Come on, Molly. We need your help! We can't do it without you." She smiles down at the pile of girl on the sidewalk.

Molly grins and says, "You mean it?"

"Yeah. Girl power. Remember?"

Molly pops up and starts running around, picking up cups that have flown everywhere. She yells at the boys, "Come on, guys! The sooner we pick everything up, the sooner we can leave."

"You heard her. Let's get to work," Rymer says with a laugh.

Rymer's dad pulls up in his car to help supervise just as they begin to gather the signs and displays. They soon realize that cleaning up at the end of the day isn't nearly as fun as setting up at the start of the day. Everything is a sticky, dirty mess. There are napkins and bits of crushed cups flying everywhere. Lemonade is all over the ground, so the bottoms of their shoes are sticky and covered in little bits of grass, sticks, and tiny rocks. They all make clicking sounds on the pavement when they walk around. And all their signs look … well, sad.

Rymer and Ash gather up the signs, and Ollie groans as he picks up napkins. Nia is picking up ice off the ground and stops to put an ice cube to her forehead. She sighs happily as the ice melts on her face.

"Why do I have to work so hard if Nia is just sitting there?" Ollie complains.

"Hey, I'm hot! The ice cools me off. Also, Ash took forever to go to the bathroom a few minutes ago, and we were all here working. You didn't yell at him!" Nia responds angrily.

"Come on! Molly has picked up like six cups in this whole time!" says Rymer.

"I'm helping! You are just walking around in circles," Molly yells.

Rymer's dad laughs as he lifts the whole stand onto the sidewalk. "You know that the more you fight, the longer it takes, right?" he says with a big grin.

"Yeah," they all mumble, guilty. They finally just cram everything in a big, wet jumble back onto the wagon and decide to sort it out later.

Rymer's dad adds, "Let's not lose your money jar. We need to see how much you made today."

Ollie whines, "I'm so exhausted that I can't even keep my eyes open. Do we have to count it tonight?"

"Let's just do it in the treehouse tomorrow after lunch," Rymer says.

"Yeah," Nia agrees. "I think I'm going to sleep for a hundred hours tonight."

They smile half-heartedly at her little joke, but they are too tired even to laugh.

Rymer's dad stops for a minute. "Hey, everyone. I think we have all earned some pool time. What do you think? Do you all want to come to our house for a swim before dinner?" The kids suddenly have a burst of energy and whoop out loud. They run down the street, laughing and not noticing as their parents follow behind picking up all the remaining trash.

As soon as they get to the house, Rymer abandons the wagon and jumps right into their pool with all his clothes on.

"Cannonball!" Ollie shouts, running off the diving board and making a big splash, followed closely by Ash. Nia stands on the edge of the pool, taking off her sling and placing her samurai swords in a safe place. Just as she starts running toward the pool, Ash yells, "Wait! Nia, can you put away our money jar first? We can't afford to lose it. And we don't want the money getting all wet."

She sighs, grabs the jar, and heads to the treehouse mumbling, "I have to do everything around here." When she gets inside, she flips the beanbag over, unzips the bottom, and digs around for the Sonic the Hedgehog wallet. Nia realizes that there are too many bills and coins to fit in it, so she zips the beanbag back up and sets the jar on the ground next to it. They can worry about it tomorrow. She dashes to the edge of the treehouse and grabs the zip line, getting ready to zip to the pool when Rymer's dad calls out to the children, "Hold on now. Before you all get wet, we need to have a little chat."

He motions for them to join him at the patio table. The three soggy boys crawl out of the water, and Nia zip-lines over to the patio, mad that she is the only one still dry.

Rymer's dad asks, "How was the first official day on the job?"

"Exhausting!" they all say in unison. Then they pause for a moment and laugh. It was almost like they had planned it.

"I want you to know how proud we are of you for working as hard as you did today. I could see that you were each committed to making the lemonade stand work, and you didn't give up even when it got hot and busy and tiring. Since I'm your investor, tomorrow I want to join you in the treehouse to talk about what comes next. Is that okay with you?"

The kids all nod, glancing hopefully back to the pool.

"Okay. We'll talk then. Now go have some fun," he says as he stands to go back inside where the rest of the parents are enjoying their own grown-up time.

The kids jump back into the pool still in their clothes. But this time, Nia is in the lead.

They have a great time in the pool, and the sticky lemonade washes off. They play sharks and minnows, have a hold-your-breath competition, and do cannonballs. Ollie has the largest splash. Nia has fun whacking the boys with a pool noodle like a samurai. But they tire out pretty quickly. Finally, they all crawl out of the water and sit next to each other on the concrete to start drying off.

Rymer says, "That was a great day. We should do it again. I mean, world's best lemonade! Everyone will come back for more."

Ollie opens his mouth, but before he can say anything, Rymer adds, "And of course, everyone should keep their same jobs."

Ollie smiles and closes his mouth.

Ash says, "That was the best first day on the job ever. I can't wait to be millionaires!"

"If we sold lemonade every day, we'd definitely become millionaires," says Rymer. "And we wouldn't have to go to school anymore!"

CHAPTER 12

INVESTOR PAYBACK

When they meet together the next day, Nia has to spend some time with her family, and Molly has lost all interest. It's just the boys today. Rymer's dad keeps his promise and joins them in the treehouse. He patiently waits while they count out all the sticky bills and coins. When they are done, he says, "So how much did you make yesterday? It looks like you did pretty good."

With a shrug, Ollie turns his calculator around so they can all see. "We made $44.75. That's not even enough to pay back our loan!" He slides back in his chair, defeated.

Rymer's dad smiles at him and flips through a few screens on his phone. "Ah," he says. "Here we go." He turns his phone around so everyone can see. In bright green letters, it says, "Congratulations, you received $206.00."

They almost fall out of their chairs, yelling, "No way! We made so much money! It actually worked! Wait until Nia hears about this!"

Ollie does a quick calculation and says, "That means we have over $500!"

"Hold on," Rymer's dad says. "This is a true business venture, so I still have to take my investment back. You owe me $48.93, remember? If I take that out of your profits, that means you now have $481.75 to put toward your gaming system."

The kids don't mind too much. The investment was fair, and it helped them get so much closer to their goal. He smiles and puts his phone in his pocket. "So are you going to do it again?"

They all nod enthusiastically.

"Why wouldn't we do it again? It's the world's best lemonade," says Rymer, feeling very grown up. "And of course, everyone will come back out for it again. We can go back tomorrow to the same spot. It's all about branding, right?"

"Yeah. It's our territory," says Ollie, waving his hands around like he owns everything around him. They high-five.

"Hold on there," Rymer's dad interrupts. "I have a little bad news. You did great at the lemonade stand, but you guys really left a big mess, and the neighbors complained. Last night, Ash's parents asked me to tell you that you can't have it in their driveway anymore. You'll have to think of something else. And your lemonade stand is in no shape to be reused until you do some serious work on it. If I were you, I'd get started on that first. Sorry, guys."

After stashing their money in their secret, hidden beanbag wallet, the boys go to the garage to look at the wagon. Rymer's dad was right. How did it get so messy? It's a disaster. The signs need repairs, and they are nearly out of supplies.

"Maybe we should take the day off," says Ash.

"Yeah. We should get the girls to help us clean the wagon," says Rymer.

They know they have enough money to reload their supplies, and they are confident they can do a better job next time. They just need to figure out where to do it.

"I've got the best idea," Ollie says. "Let's go to the beach where it's really hot and sell there."

"Good idea … in theory," says Ash, "but everyone knows that wind and sand don't mix well with lemonade. Remember how windy it was yesterday?"

"Wait a second!" Rymer says. "I have a better idea! Let's set up the stand here at my house but let the customers pick their lemons and squeeze their own juice. Then we don't hardly even have to do the work!"

Then they remember that they picked all the lemons, so there's nothing left for customers to pick.

"It would be cool if we could do something new and different, though," says Ash. "I'm kind of tired of the same two things. Like maybe we could sell something hot to make the refreshing lemonade sound even better? Maybe we could make grilled cheese sandwiches! No crust, of course."

"Yeah, but how on earth are we going to cook on this wagon?" says Ollie. "Not to mention, the cheese will look like plastic after it cools off."

Molly has wandered out into the garage and has been listening to them. "I'm the sugar expert, guys. Maybe you can add syrup to the sugar," she says.

"No way," says Rymer. "It will turn the lemonade brown. Duh."

Ash sighs and says, "Guys, I need a break. I think I'm going to go home for the rest of the day. Let's worry about this tomorrow."

They all go their separate ways.

The next day, they are all back together again. After a lot of effort, the wagon is cleaned up and the signs are all repaired. ROAR'N Lemonade is back in business. They decide to set up in Rymer's driveway this time. Maybe the construction workers across the road will come buy some.

"Oh, wait," Rymer says. "We are out of supplies. No lemons, no ice, no sugar, no anything!"

"What are we supposed to do?" Nia asks.

"I guess we could ask Kristi to take us to the store, but who knows when she will have time to take us again?"

They walk inside to see a pleasant surprise. Kristi has all the supplies they need to get back out there!

"Wow!" Molly exclaims.

"Hold on," Ash says. "What you gonna charge us?"

"Nothing!" Kristi says, "Um, think of it as a tip. For …" She pauses, thinking for a moment. "Great effort. You guys are really giving it everything you can out there, and I'm proud of you."

She gives Rymer a tight hug and sends them on their way with their arms full of everything they need.

"I still think it would be a fun idea to have everyone squeeze their own lemons," Rymer says. "Let's try that this time and see if it works."

They set up the stand and quickly realize that everyone hates squeezing lemons. After an hour, they haven't had a single paying customer. A few kids seemed interested, but when they learned they had to do it themselves, they said, "If I want to squeeze my own lemons, I'll do it at home and save my money."

Rymer sits on the ground and groans. "There is nothing cute about this. We are losing time, and every business tycoon knows that time is money."

"Yeah, not even the old ladies will buy some. And they all think we're adorable!" Ollie says.

"Wait, here comes one now. Everyone, stations!" Rymer yells.

"Come on, guys. It's just my grandma," Nia says. She smiles and welcomes her to ROAR'N Lemonade.

"Oh, honey," her grandma says. "I've been watching you from the bench over there, and I think this new idea of yours isn't working like you had planned it."

The kids are all listening, hoping she is going to say she will buy some lemonade after all.

"I know you hate squeezing lemons, but so do the costumers. I think you've learned this by now, and I think I have the solution to your problem. It is called the Samurai Squeezer. It is an automatic juicer that I think could really help. Come over to our house tomorrow."

"Wow!" Ash says. "Imagine how much easier that will make our life!"

Nia hugs her grandma. "Thank you so much! This is amazing!"

As the kids put everything away, they know that with their newfound juicer, the TV and gaming system are as good as theirs. They just need to figure out where to go.

CHAPTER 13

THE BIG BREAK

They decide to close the stand the next day so they can figure out how the juicer works. They are gathered in Nia's kitchen when her dad walks through the kitchen to the living room and asks what they are doing.

"Figuring out our new weapon and deciding a plan of attack!" says Ollie, hitting a superhero pose. "Whooooo-aaaa!"

"Where did your grandma even find this?" asks Ash.

"Yeah, I've never seen anything like this," says Rymer. "Was it passed down from your lemonade-making samurai ancestors?" He slices the air with a pretend sword and says, "Shweeee. Shwooo."

Nia laughs and answers, "I think she probably just bought it somewhere because my dad had a lemonade stand like us when he was little."

They experiment with it for a while, getting excited every time they crush another lemon. The juice goes into a cup, and the pulp and seeds plop into a small container on the side. It's so easy! After a while, they think they have the hang of it, so they start to clean everything up.

"This is great and all," says Rymer. "But we still don't have a place to sell lemonade."

Suddenly Ash blurts out, "Ah! Ah! There-za … there-za … ah!"

Ollie asks, "Are you okay, Ash? Did you swallow a bug or something?"

"No! Nia! Get your dad's phone," Ash says urgently.

She nods and runs into the living room yelling, "Dad! I need your phone! Now! It's a business emergency!"

The boys can hear him respond, "Okay, okay. You can use it for your business, but I want it right back when you're done. And be careful not to get lemon juice on it."

Nia runs back into the kitchen and hands Ash the phone. He takes a deep breath and says in one long rush, "There is a golf tournament happening tomorrow—this is the perfect opportunity for us to earn the rest of the money before school starts—you know my family likes to go golfing, and my parents told me about it last night, and it seemed to me like the perfect place to sell lemonade because you remember how hot it got out there when we were there getting balls, but I forgot about it until just now!"

Everyone grins from ear to ear. This could be the ticket to earn them all the money they need. If they do it correctly.

"Now that we have this juicer, making lemonade will be way easier," Ash says. "The perfect weapon for a perfect plan."

Because the golf tournament is the next day, they spend the rest of the day making sure they are ready to sell there. Rymer goes home and talks to his dad about it, and he is very supportive of them setting up their stand there, and he contacts the coordinator of the event to make sure they are allowed to be vendors. He also says it may be a good idea if there is at least one adult to watch and help them if anything goes wrong. The kids set up a schedule with all their parents taking a shift to help them out.

At 6:00 a.m. the next day, they all meet at Rymer's house and hit the road with the wagon. None of them can remember the last time

they were up this early! But it doesn't matter. They all are so pumped up that they can barely contain themselves. They pull their wagon down the road as the sun starts to rise, talking loudly and excitedly as they go.

Rymer's dad took care of the paperwork for them, but when they get there, the event coordinator makes sure to have each of the kids sign their names to the contract ... even Molly. Then he explains that as vendors, they need to stay until 1:00 p.m., and they will be charged $100 to use a space on the course. Ollie was ready for this and pulls the Sonic wallet out of his pocket and pays the money just like a grown-up. He makes a note in a little notebook that he brought to keep track of their earnings. They now need to earn $836.18 to make it to their goal.

As they look around, they see that there are thousands of fans at the tournament. Each hole has various concession stands, some with just drinks, some with food and drinks, some with golf gear and clothing for sale. There seem to be private parties at a few of the homes that line the course, and Rymer's dad explains that they are called "hospitality" or "sponsor" events. There are even booths with fun stuff like golf simulators and little putting greens in them.

The biggest tent has the name "Smellinger Supply" across it in big blue letters with "VIP TENT" in gold letters below that. It is at the eighteenth hole and is sponsored by Howard Smellinger, the owner of the largest fishing supply and bait shop on the island. Everyone knows Smellinger's. The kids set up their stand near this VIP tent.

As they work, Rymer thinks the golf fans are hilarious. Some look like normal people, dressed like you would expect in khaki shorts and polos. Some are all decked out in golf apparel. Lots of kids have on hats with autographs all over them. One thing they all have in common is they are hot, thirsty, and pushy.

The kids all fall into their roles without any trouble as they begin selling their lemonade. They have their signs and their Samurai Squeezer, so they are prepared for a big day.

At 7:00 a.m., the tournament officially begins, and the orders start to pour in. So many orders! It's already getting hot and humid outside, and everyone is looking for ways to keep cool.

As the day goes on, the crowds get pretty big. There are some awfully sunburnt people and lots of sweaty older men with big bellies and older ladies with funny visors on. The kids make sure to be really nice to the ladies in the visors because they tend to tip the best. They are taking cash and virtual payments with ease now. It seems like everyone at the tournament wants some of their lemonade!

The calculator does not leave Ollie's side during business hours. He's obsessed with numbers now and can't help running every calculation he can think of, like how many lemonades they have to sell to get their hundred-dollar fee back and how much sugar they can buy with ten dollars.

At 9:30 a.m., the kids realize they have almost run out of supplies. They decide to go talk to the grumpy golf manager to see if he will allow them to save their spot while they make another run to the store with Ollie's mom, who is there with them. He says no and tries to kick them out. They protest that they are just kids and that they will only be gone for a few minutes.

He huffs, "You should have come prepared. If you have run out of product, you have no place on this course. I remember you. You were here a few days ago fishing in the pond. I've had just about enough of this. I think it's time for you all to pack up and leave."

Just then, a big man who was in the middle of purchasing two of the last cups of lemonade for himself and his daughter steps in. "I couldn't help overhearing the conversation," he says. "I'm Howard Smellinger, and this is the best lemonade I've ever tasted."

"Well, it is the world's best lemonade," says Rymer with his sleeves rolled up and his finger pointing straight up in a number one. The gang agrees and simultaneously says, "Duh."

Mr. Smellinger turns to the manager and continues. "If you make these kids leave the tournament, I'll never sponsor it again. I want them to be my guests for the rest of the tournament. In fact, they can hang out in my VIP tent for as long as they want! I would also like to pay their registration fee of $100 and book them to serve their delicious lemonade at my daughter's birthday next week!"

He then turns to the kids and says, "Roar!"

"N," says Nia. "It's 'ROAR'N'!"

The kids go crazy as Mr. Smellinger hands them $100 to cover their registration fee and offers them $250 for the birthday party. He continues, "If it's as good at the birthday party as it was here, I'll let you sell it in my fishing supply and bait shop whenever you want!"

Fans nearby erupt in cheers and pat the kids on their backs, high-five them, and start chanting, "ROAR'N! ROAR'N!" It's the best moment of their lives.

They finish up selling the rest of their lemonade and then close the stand to hang out in the VIP tent for the rest of the tournament. The kids have become instant celebrities.

CHAPTER 14

SUCCESS!

Completely exhausted from a long and happy day, the kids stumble home dragging their tired wagon behind them. They decide they better count their earnings before they all leave. They are stunned to realize that they have earned $553.25 in cash. And Rymer's dad shows them how much they got from virtual payments—$750! That's a total of $1,303.25, which is almost enough to buy the TV and the gaming system without even adding it to what they have already saved.

Ollie does a quick calculation and says, "You'll never believe this, guys. We have $1,685! That's more than $200 over what we need!"

Completely satisfied, they all go home and immediately fall asleep.

It's the weekend, so the kids meet together after lunch the next day, and Rymer nags his dad and stepmom to take them all to the store. They are way too excited to wait for something in the mail, so they have agreed to go to a huge electronics store where they have all the consoles hooked up to massive TVs with the latest games on them to sample along with colorful controllers, headsets, and even gaming chairs to sit in with speakers and multiple screens. After what seems like forever to get everyone's shoes on and loaded in the car, they all go to the store together.

They play for a while and debate all their options before they finally choose a console that comes with two games from a selection of a few that are pretty popular, and they take a group vote on the games. They agree that they will only buy games that are multiplayer so they all get turns to play together. The kids are overjoyed, jumping all over as they check out. The cashier notices their energy and grins as she rings up their purchase and takes their money, some of it still sticky with lemonade.

They jump in the car, and Ollie says, "We should have an unboxing party tonight and invite everyone in the neighborhood who helped us reach our goal."

As usual, most of them agree, so when they get back to Rymer's house, they make flyers and start distributing them to all the other kids in the neighborhood. Rymer's parents think it's a great idea to have an end-of-summer block party, so they volunteer to help get snacks and drinks while the kids get the word out.

The party starts after dinner, and kids start to trickle into the backyard followed by grown-ups. There are lights up and a snack table by the pool. The gang's parents are really surprised that their children could restrain themselves for this long. The party is doing well, and people are in the pool, going down the zip line, and there is music that some of the older kids are dancing to. Even Rymer's big brothers are in a great mood.

Ollie finds another dead moth in his pocket and takes this as an opportunity to have a tiny little funeral for it, burying it under the lemon tree with a couple of the younger kids. After they are done and go back to the snack table, Nia's dog Terrence digs it up and eats it, but nobody notices.

Rymer decides it's time for the unboxing and tries to get everyone to gather around the patio, where the boxes from the store are sitting. Every time he yells for people to come over, the crowd just gets louder to talk over him. Molly sees what is going on and climbs up on the middle of the snack table and lets out a scream.

"Everyone stop what you're doing and listen!" she yells to the stunned crowd. "Rymer has something to say," she adds as she climbs back down.

Rymer laughs and says, "Thank you, Molly. It's time for the big event, everyone. Drumroll, please!"

As everyone makes a drumroll sound, Nia slices through the tape that holds the boxes together, and the kids finally unbox their gaming system and television. Some of the dads help them set it all up in the treehouse, and everyone begins taking turns playing some video games. Moms, dads, siblings, and neighbors all have a great time. By the time the party ends, people leave with smiles on their faces.

The gang sits on the edge of the pool, dangling their feet in the water. "I will be happy if I never see another glass of lemonade again," says Ollie.

"I wouldn't mind," says Rymer. "It's what got us this awesome setup."

"We got that awesome setup," Ash corrects him. "Lemonade was the tool that got us there."

The kids are quiet for a moment until Nia says, "It was kind of fun, wasn't it?"

The next weekend, they all meet one more time at Rymer's house to get the stand all set up for Mr. Smellinger's daughter's birthday party. It's on the other side of the island, so they have to load everything up in Rymer's dad's car. They all pile in and put on some music on the radio, and they all sing loudly during the short drive. Even Rymer's dad sings along.

When they get there, they start setting everything up and say hi to Mr. Smellinger and his daughter. He says, "You can set up inside my house because it's so hot. I think you'll stay cooler in there. We've cleared out a space in the dining room for you, and there are even some chairs you can use to relax."

They haul the wagon (with some grown-up help) into the dining room and set up all the cups and pitchers. They don't need their signs this time, so they leave those in the car.

Mr. Smellinger's daughter is really excited to have the world's best lemonade stand at her seventh birthday party! And she has kid chefs there to make it right in front of them. They are like little celebrities after the golf tournament, and everyone on the island knows them. They were even in the newspaper.

When her friends all get there, they recognize Rymer, Ash, Ollie, and Nia and are amazed. After they cut the cake, the birthday party kids all go outside playing games, and they keep running back inside to drink more lemonade. Since they aren't worried about taking money or waving signs, they all put in a lot of effort to keep things clean and organized. Nobody spills lemonade this time, and they aren't even getting sticky.

By the end of the party, parents start to show up to collect their kids. One of the fathers sees the stand and asks for a cup. He says, "Wow! This is the best lemonade I have ever had!"

"World's best!" says Rymer.

"You know, I'm in the beverage bottling business, and I think this could be a terrific new product. I'd like to talk to you and your parents about going into business together." He hands his business card to Rymer's dad and says, "Call me."

A few months later, the treehouse looks a little different. They have renamed it Lemonade House, and pictures of the golf tournament hang on the wall. There is a newspaper clipping about their business and how they were invited to the VIP tent and hailed as heroes.

Their old wagon sits in the corner, filled with cans of ROAR'N Lemonade. Boxes with the same label sit at the base of the treehouse, ready to be sold. On the back patio of Rymer's house is a vending machine with every button containing ROAR'N Lemonade cans.

As usual, Rymer, Ollie, Ash, and Nia are in their treehouse playing video games. Ash says, "You know, I kind of like this business stuff."

Rymer concentrates on getting his in-game character to jump across a canyon. "Yeah, we're on our way to becoming millionaires. Just like I always said!"

CPSIA information can be obtained
at www.ICGtesting.com
Printed in the USA
BVHW040746090523
663835BV00015B/362/J

9 798887 501123